RECKLESS REBOUND

USA TODAY BESTSELLING AUTHOR

BROOKE O'BRIEN

Reckless Rebound is a standalone story inspired by Vi Keeland and Penelope Ward's Playboy Pilot. It's published as part of the Cocky Hero Club world, a series of original works, written by various authors, and inspired by Keeland and Ward's *New York Times* bestselling series.

MEN OF BLAZE SERIES
READING ORDER

PERSONAL FOUL

a coach's daughter, workplace, basketball sports romance

RECKLESS REBOUND

A Men of Blaze and Cocky Hero Club crossover
a bad boy surprise pregnancy, basketball sports romance

Learn more and purchase your copy at:
www.authorbrookeobrien.com/menofblaze

PROLOGUE

JAXSEN WILD SUSPENDED FOR SHOVING CREW SAVAGE

Miami Blaze guard, Jaxsen Wild, was suspended for three games and will be sidelined without pay going into the playoffs, the Basketball League Association reported on Thursday.

Wild was ejected from the game vs. Chicago after shoving Crew Savage. The outburst came after Savage shot and made a three-pointer, then threw his hands up, taunting Wild.

The two exchanged words on the court, sparking frustration from Wild before he pushed Savage, knocking him to the ground.

Many speculate what this could mean for Wild as he moves into the post-season, his head clearly not in the right place following their loss to San Antonio. With his contract playing for Miami up for renewal this fall, it's believed this could be the end of his reign playing for the Blaze, and many are wondering who would want to pick him up.

His defensive play has led to a few too many aggressive outbursts on the court. After six years in the league, he still hasn't managed to make it to the finals; could it be time for him to hang up his jersey, or can he get his head back in the game and lead his team to a championship?

CHAPTER ONE

JAXSEN

"Keep your mouth shut and leave the talking to me, all right?" Adrian grumbles under his breath.

He pushes the conference room door open, turning to shoot me one last warning look. I clench my jaw, strolling past him, and resist the urge to roll my eyes.

I've always hated meetings with these big wigs. All they care about is a payout. Sitting on their high and mighty throne, looking down their nose at me and everyone else.

They should be thanking *me*.

I get it. I put their precious Crew Savage at risk of being injured. At the end of the day, it drew in attention and had the media losing their ever-loving minds, leading to more viewers. *Cha-ching!* More money for them.

I stride into the room and pull out a chair, then take a seat in the middle of the boardroom table. Across from me are three men dressed in suits and ties. Gray and silver strands pepper their hair and face, marking the end of their time in the league.

I'm dressed and ready to play the part too. If I need to come in here and bite my tongue, show I'm remorseful and willing to take the slap on the wrist, I will. It's a means to an end.

That's all this meeting is too. What I care about is getting back on the court and winning a championship.

"Thank you for being here today," Alex Steele, the league commissioner, says. His eyes scan the room before narrowing on mine.

I grit my teeth and nod, tapping my fingers along the table while I wait for him to continue.

A buxom blonde sits at the end of the table with a laptop positioned in front of her. Her fingers click as she furiously types across the keyboard, presumably taking notes. The sound of the clacking is like nails on a chalkboard, grating on my already frayed nerves.

"It should come as no surprise to you, Mr. Wild, why we've asked you to be here today."

I nod, but my face remains stoic.

I want to keep playing basketball. I've busted my ass over the years to be one of the best defensive players in the league.

I didn't get here by puckering up and kissing asses, and I certainly wasn't going to start today.

"This is your third ejection this season. Each one has been more reckless than the one before."

I flare my nostrils and grind my teeth. As much as I hate to admit it, he's right.

I've begun to let shit get out of hand. Some of these guys know what to say and do to get under my skin, and I've let my reaction put my career in jeopardy.

"You've become a liability to your team, to the players, and this organization."

"Oh, the players." I scoff. "What about Savage, though, huh? The fucker gets off taunting me every time, making bullshit comments under his breath, yet the refs always seem to turn a blind eye to him."

Adrian's hand darts out from where he sits next to me, pushing my chest back, attempting to calm me down. Alex shakes his head and glances over to one of the guys next to him as if they expected for this outburst to happen.

"Chill the fuck out, will ya?" Adrian mutters under his breath. It's a subtle reminder I don't want the conversation to play out this way.

I sigh and shake my head.

I'm sick of players like Crew Savage who intentionally go out there pulling cheap shots, flopping for the sake of getting to the free-throw line, and causing unnecessary fouls.

He's always getting away with it, and then players like me who won't put up with it are made out to look like the bad guy.

Savage's clock has been ticking. He's had it coming, and I can't wait for the chance to face him again, this time in the playoffs.

Only this time, I am going to put up and shut his ass up.

"Mr. Steele, we come to you today ready to discuss options in how we can address this. Jaxsen recognizes the harm behind his actions, and he's prepared to face the consequences without risking his career or position with the Miami Blaze," Adrian says.

"I can't speak for the Blaze, Mr. Wild. Your future with the Blaze will be left to them when your contract is up for renewal in September. However, as I've mentioned, keeping you in the league has become a liability. I want to be very clear with you, we will not tolerate this sort of outburst in the future. If this behavior continues, please be prepared, you could be removed from the league entirely. Do I make myself clear?"

I grit my teeth and nod, knowing what's on the line if I say what's truly on my mind. "Understood."

He stares at me for a long moment, and I maintain his eye contact the entire time.

"Very well," he states. "As we've discussed previously, you'll be suspended for the next three games, which means you'll miss the start of the playoffs. This suspension includes loss of pay, along with a fine of $50,000."

Ouch.

They wanted to send a message, and it was heard loud and clear.

"You're a talented young man with a bright future ahead of you—if you get your shit together. I strongly encourage you to take this time to reflect on your actions, and when you return to the court, you come back the man your team, coaches, and the rest of the organization knows you can be."

Those are nearly the same words my mother uses every time I've been ejected. I'm too talented for this, this isn't the man she raised me to be, and I'm better than letting other players get to me.

She is right. Steele is right.

"Understood, sir." I nod.

My eyes flash over to the blonde again, and her eyes are already on me as if she was waiting for the moment I looked her way. She runs her tongue along her lower lip and presses her lips together, puckering them. She adjusts her posture, forcing her breasts out further, and I want to roll my eyes.

I'm used to women like her who flock to players in the league. There's no shortage of them back in Miami either. They all hang around at Blazin' Shooters, the local sports bar where a lot of the players hang out in our downtime.

They strut past us with their fake tits spilling over their too-small tops, short shorts, and high heels, thinking we'll be drooling over ourselves to take them home.

Been there, done that one.

If there's anything all this has taught me, it's I need to get my act together and focus on our chance of winning a ring.

After I'm done listening to them chastise me like a child, I'm ready to get my ass out of there and on the first flight back to Miami.

"You stayin' in town tonight or heading back home?" Adrian asks, as we push through the doors, heading out to the SUV waiting for us outside.

The wind swirls around us, whipping us into a cloud of large snowflakes. The storm appears to be hitting sooner than expected. I can only hope we get off the ground before the conditions worsen.

Despite the whiteout conditions, there's still a line of paparazzi waiting for us like vultures ready to pounce. I put my aviators on to shield my eyes and duck my head, hurrying to the open door waiting for me.

"Goddamn, I swear they're worse here than they are in Miami."

Adrian chuckles as he climbs in next to me. The driver quickly pulls out, veering onto the busy streets of New York City.

"I booked my flight earlier in case the storm hit. I want to get out of here as soon as I can."

"I'll ride with ya to the airport. I have a few things to talk to you about."

I adjust myself into the seat, needing room to spread my legs in this cramped backseat, and stare out the window at the snow coming down. It's thick, already starting to pile up in the short time we were in our meeting.

These freezing temperatures are something I'm not used to, having grown up in Georgia before I was drafted to play for the Miami Blaze.

I've traveled for games and hit the colder weather, but I've never experienced anything like this. It's hard to see out the windshield, which makes me anxious thinking about what this could mean for my flight.

I need an act of God if I have any hope of getting out of here without my flight being canceled.

"The meeting didn't go as we expected, but certainly better than it could've."

I roll my eyes and rest my chin on my closed fist, not bothering to look in his direction.

"Jaxsen, Steele is right, man. You need to get your shit together, or you're gonna lose everything you've busted your ass for."

I don't want to hear it from him too, but it is different when it comes from Adrian. He's less of my manager and has grown to be more of a friend over the years. I trust him and his opinions. He has my best interests in mind, but damn it if I don't want to tell him to shove it up his ass sometimes.

"When you get back home, I think you should lay low. Stay out of the clubs and bars, all right? Get back in the gym, focus on getting your mind and body right. The playoffs are around the corner, and you need to be on your A-game."

I nod. I don't have time to think about anything else if I want to get my team to the finals.

"Don't stress about the contract or media bullshit, though, okay? I'll take care of it. I just need you to keep a low profile. Once we get through the end of the season, things will start to settle, and everyone will quit breathing down your neck."

The downside to living life in the public eye is you can never tell who you can trust.

I've learned the hard way with friends and relationships who only wanted a piece of Jaxsen for the money or success I could bring with it.

After having my name run through the mud in gossip articles one too many times, I've given up on dating. I'd rather be single forever, with a string of one-night stands left in my wake, than deal with the drama ever again.

It doesn't matter anymore, though. I have the playoffs in my future and need to get my head on straight if I have any hope of saving my career.

I'm Jaxsen fuckin' Wild.

The last thing I'm gonna do is let anyone take what I've worked so hard to build.

CHAPTER TWO

EMMY

"Well, well, well. Would you look what the cat dragged in." Cody snickers.

I speed walk through the hotel lobby, my suitcase damn near tipping over in my race to make it on time. I frantically rake my hand through my hair, attempting to tame the unruly strands, while mentally running through the list of things I needed to grab on my way out the door.

I hope like hell I didn't leave anything behind because I have no time to go back now.

"It's not what you think," I grumble under my breath.

I follow behind my best friend and the rest of the crew out toward the van waiting to shuttle us to the airport.

The temperatures dropped significantly overnight. Judging by the amount of snow, we'll be lucky if Carter can get us off the ground as planned.

"What happened?" Cody quirks his brow, picking up the concern in my voice.

"Matthew is what happened," I hiss. "He wouldn't stop calling last night. I turned my phone off in the midst of my frustration, hoping to catch a couple hours of sleep."

Cody rolls his eyes and climbs into the backseat, and I claim the spot next to him before pulling the door shut behind me.

"I swear to God, if I ever see that man again ..." He huffs out an exasperated sigh. I grin at the sound of the twang in his voice showing off his southern roots.

His sass is what we bonded over in the beginning and made us such close friends. We were either going to love or hate each other; there would be no in-between.

We met through my sister when she helped land me the job working for International Airlines. They were able to work around my school schedule, putting me on the weekend rotation between Chicago, Miami, and New York.

As a fashion design student, I dreaded the thought of wearing their horrid flight attendant uniform, but I couldn't pass up the money. Not to mention, who wouldn't love the chance to travel for free?

I'm thankful our hotel isn't too far from the airport, and we're able to make the drive without any issues from the weather. We even have some time to spare before passengers start to board.

"What did he say last night?" Cody asks, breaking the silence.

Cody was never a fan of my ex-boyfriend. He suspected Matthew was up to something behind my back when we were together back home in Chicago and he was ignoring my calls constantly.

I couldn't deny it anymore; Cody was right. Since we broke up, I've started to realize all the red flags I saw were there, but chose to ignore, not wanting to believe he would hurt me.

"He's back to making excuses. He had the nerve to say it was an old account and he hasn't used it since we started dating." I smirk, chuckling under my breath at the audacity.

We pull up under the awning and begin to unload.

"Old account?" Cody scoffs. "Does he seriously think you're gonna believe some bullshit like that?"

A friend of mine reached out to me after seeing him on a dating app. There's still an ache in my chest when I think about how naïve I was for so long.

My heart dropped to the pit of my stomach when she sent me the photos, including one of us when we went fishing down by Navy Pier. He had the audacity to use one of the photos I took from our day together only to turn around and try to claim it was an old account from before we dated.

The portico along the front of the entrance helps shield us from the falling snow as we hurry to grab our bags. We're in the middle of talking when a black SUV pulls up behind us at the terminal and a tall man climbs out of the backseat.

He's wearing dark aviators covering his eyes, his hair is light brown, buzzed short on the sides and longer on the top. It's styled in a messy look as if he ran his hand through it and it laid perfectly that way. His skin is tan as if he's ready to get back to whatever tropical location he's from, with a suit fitting him like it was made perfectly for him.

"Damnnn," Cody mumbles under his breath.

Except quiet and Cody are two things that don't go together.

The driver of the car hands the stranger his suitcase when he shifts his gaze toward us, jolting me out of my trace.

"I think he heard you," I whisper, chastising Cody. He doesn't seem to care, flashing the man a broad smile while he subtly shrugs his shoulders.

"I still say you need to get back at him for what he did to you," Cody says, changing the subject back to Matthew. "Men like him shouldn't be able to pull such heinous crimes and get away with it."

I laugh, nearly folding in half. "What? You mean sending him a bouquet of Get Well Soon balloons with a card saying, 'Dear Matthew, sorry about your dick' isn't enough for you?"

"Not even close." He shakes his head and smirks. "It seems appropriate after he slipped and fell, only to have his dick land inside his *friend*." He rolls his eyes, accentuating the word friend.

"I still can't believe I fell for the whole *just friends* line."

We both reach for the handle of our suitcases, following the line of people scurrying to get into the airport.

"You deserve so much better," Cody adds.

The smell of deep sandalwood cologne permeates the air around me, and I glance over to find Mr. Tall, Tan, and Dreamy standing behind me. He glances down, noticing me staring, but his face remains indifferent.

His cold exterior has me curling my lip and twisting back around.

Red flag.

The last thing I need is another man who's full of himself catching my attention. I'm still trying to move on from the last one who screwed me over.

"Do you think there's any chance our flight will get delayed?" I mutter to Cody.

"I hope not, but I wouldn't mind either."

I dart my eyes over to him and he winks.

He's up to something, and I can only imagine what it could be.

"You never did tell me where *you* were last night. I sent you a text before I crawled into bed, and you never responded back."

He bites his lip and glances at me out of the corner of his eye.

"What the hell did you do?"

"I don't kiss and tell, sweetie."

"Oh, good to know. I'll remember that the next time you try to pry your way into my business."

"Don't even get me started, Ms. Thang," he retorts. "I was spending time with a friend is all. There's nothing to tell."

"Oh, a friend." I smirk. "Why? Was he not any good?" I giggle.

The sound of a throat clearing behind me sends both of our heads jolting over our shoulders. Mr. Dreamy purses his lips together but otherwise keeps his face hard as stone.

"Boy, would I love to crack that man's shell, though," he whispers before he whistles. I smack him on the arm and pull Cody over to the side, letting him pass by us.

He's clearly not amused by our side chatter through the airport.

He stalks past us, giving us both the chance to check out his ass. I shake my head. I need to focus, or we're going to be late.

"I'm gonna jet to the bathroom quick to freshen up."

"Try to hurry or Carter is gonna be ticked. Remember how he handled it the last time?"

"Don't remind me," I laugh. "I'll meet you at the Sky Lounge," I holler over my shoulder, dragging my suitcase with me while I hurry toward the bathrooms.

Carter can chill. He's one of the pilots for International Airlines and a longtime friend of my sister, Alexa. They have a past together, so while I may get on his nerves from time to time, he tends to regard me like a sister too. He gets annoyed but moves on from it quickly.

Thankfully, there's no line at the bathrooms. I run into an open stall toward the end and unzip my suitcase, quickly pulling out my uniform. It takes me a few minutes to get it on, slowly rolling on my nylons before stepping into my high heel pumps.

Once I finish, I quickly wash my hands and fix my hair before putting the finishing touches on my makeup. There's still a little left over from the night before.

I grit my teeth in annoyance, wishing I had a chance to shower and get ready this morning.

I'm too busy trying to hurry so I can catch up to Cody when I come barreling out the door and crash into a hard chest. My suitcase falls to the ground at my feet, but I'm too distracted to care.

His scent is what hits me first, nearly causing me to stumble over my feet, when his long arm swoops around my waist to hold me up. I slowly trail my eyes over his neatly pressed suit to meet his.

He's no longer wearing his sunglasses, giving me a glimpse of his beautiful crystal-blue eyes. He has long eyelashes and a dimple on his cheek, which does crazy things to my heart.

"You should pay more attention to where you're walking so you don't run into people."

His voice is deep and gravely. His comment was meant as a subtle dig at the fact I was checking him out earlier. I curl my lip in disgust.

"You were more attractive before you opened your mouth."

His brows shoot up and he clenches his jaw.

I bend down and reach for the handle of my suitcase before turning away from him. He clears his throat again, stopping me in my tracks. I pause, glancing over my shoulder.

"What?"

"No apology?" he asks, but I choose to ignore the question.

"You're forgiven."

He smirks, running his hand over his jaw. He adjusts the watch on his wrist.

I wait to see if he has any other rude comments to add before I take off.

"Fine," I sigh, realizing I'm at work. "I'm sorry for not seeing you there and for running into you. Better? Now, if you'll excuse me, I need to get going."

He nods. I roll my eyes, this time making it clear I'm equally as annoyed as he is. I'm a few feet away from him when I hear him say, "I was hoping for a card or some balloons, but you're forgiven."

I chuckle under my breath and shake my head. I hear his laughter behind me but don't bother turning around again.

I've let one asshole make me late this morning. I'm not gonna add another to the list.

CHAPTER THREE

EMMY

"Damn, I thought you got lost. I was about to come searching for you." Cody smirks.

I shake my head. "Lost? I've been to this airport a million times. How would I end up lost?"

"Lost. Missing. Something. You said you were going to freshen up, not disappear."

"No, but you'll never guess who I ran into when I went to the bathroom."

"Who?" His brows shoot up.

"The guy we saw outside. Mr. Tall, Tan, and Dreamy."

"He was in the bathroom?" he barks out.

"No," I snort. "I literally ran into him as I was rushing out and slammed right into him."

A slow smile stretches across his face. "You did, did you?"

I shake my head and hold my hands up in surrender. "He was an asshole about the whole thing too."

Carter, who's sitting at the table next to us, is staring between the two of us. His eyes bounce back and forth, trying to follow our conversation. He furrows his brows and shakes his head before turning his attention back to his laptop in front of him.

"Any news on this storm rolling in? You think we'll get up in the air before it gets too bad that we're stuck here?"

"I don't know." He releases a puff of air. "It's not looking good. I've been keeping an eye on the weather, and they're saying the east coast is supposed to get hit hard. We could get delayed for a day, maybe even two."

My heart sinks. I don't want to be stuck here for another night, but it's not the worst thing in the world either. I just want to get back home to Chicago. I have a ton of homework to catch up on.

I recently applied and interviewed for an internship working for a designer, Michael Jacobs. I was able to land three letters of recommendation from designers and a teacher I've worked with previously, helping bolster my chances. I'm hoping to hear back soon.

If I got it, I'd be spending the summer in Miami while splitting my time working for the airline.

After the breakup, I could use all the distraction I can get. This would add a lot to my plate, but it's an opportunity of a lifetime and a chance I can't pass up.

It's been my dream to work in fashion since I was young. I used to constantly dig around in my mom's closet, admiring and trying on her designer dresses and custom jewelry.

To have the chance to work alongside Michael Jacobs and network amongst some of the best in the business would give me an incredible start in the industry.

I'm still waiting to hear back from them, but they said they'd be in touch soon.

We start to board the plane. I'm scheduled with Cody to cover first class.

"Did you see who's on the flight with us?" Cody bumps his shoulder against mine, nodding his head toward the corner where I see Mr. Dreamy.

He's seated along the aisle; the spot next to him near the window is left open. He's too busy staring out the window to pay us any mind.

The snow outside is still coming down fast, and the wind has begun picking up. Every time I look outside, I get a little more anxious, wishing we could get off the ground. It's only a matter of time before they start calling off flights, which would mean we'd be stuck here until at least the morning.

Cody looks at me before his eyes flash over to an older couple boarding the plane, greeting them with a warm smile. Once they pass by us and find their seat, he turns back to me.

His voice drops low. "The things I'd do to that man would be considered indecent and criminal."

I snicker, shaking my head. My gaze slowly trails back over to him, only this time his eyes are on the two of us. The sight of his blue eyes again nearly sucks all the air from my lungs.

Cody reaches for the phone to the PA system and holds it to his mouth before muttering, "If you don't want him, I'm calling dibs." He winks at me.

I don't notice he's pressed the button to begin the preflight announcements until I fire back my response.

"You can have him. He's an asshole," I blurt out.

All eyes from the passengers dart over to us. My cheeks burn with embarrassment, and my eyes nearly bulge out of their sockets.

"Good morning, ladies and gentlemen. Welcome to International Airlines. My name is Cody and this one, with the mouth of a sailor, is Emerson. We have JaLisa and Ashley working alongside us as well. We are your cabin crew, here to ensure you have an enjoyable flight to Miami today."

The passengers chuckle before turning their attention back to Cody. Me, on the other hand, I'm ready to hide in the cockpit.

"We're sorry for the delay in our departure today. We're still waiting for official word from Captain Carter, our pilot, on when we'll be taking off. Due to the weather, there's a possibility all flights will be canceled. While we wait, we'll make rounds to offer you some refreshments. Thank you for your patience today."

I chance a glance over at Mr. Dreamy. He must feel my gaze on him when he glances in my direction. Although I could swear there's a softness to his gaze that wasn't there before.

I shake myself out of my thoughts, reaching for the tray of beverages. Cody mutters "sorry" under his breath. I give him a reassuring smile before pushing all thoughts out of my mind.

This has been a day from hell. At this point, all I want is to crawl back into bed and sleep the day away, wake up and have a do-over.

The entire time we make our rounds, I feel his eyes burn into my skin. I do my best to avoid looking over at him, but the temptation is too thick. When I give in and look in his direction, I always find him staring back at me. The heat in his eyes sends a shiver through my body.

"Lucy in the Sky with Diamonds" begins to play over the loudspeaker. It's a part of Carter's preflight ritual, and I can't help but smile. There's something so comforting about it.

We pass out drinks and snacks to passengers, making conversation with them about their trip and the weather. My heart rate begins to pick up the closer I get to Mr. Dreamy and the chance to speak to him again.

Despite how big of an asshole he was in the beginning, I find myself eager to hear his voice again. The deep timbre does wicked things to my body.

I take the last step separating us when my foot gets caught on something beneath a seat. It would've been fine until my ankle rolls to the side, sending me nearly face planting in his lap and the tray in my hand crashing to the floor.

If I was embarrassed before, there are no words to describe how I feel now.

He reaches his hand out and grips my forearm as I push to stand. I'm ready to high-tail it off the plane and tell Cody he can cover this one on his own.

"I'm beginning to think you're intentionally looking for ways to be in my arms." He chuckles. His voice is low enough for only me to hear.

It takes a second for his words to sink in, needing a moment to come down from the high of hearing his voice.

"Of course, you would." I laugh, shaking my head as I push myself up.

"I'm down for it, if you are."

I suck in a quick breath. He's one of those guys who knows how attractive he is, and I can't tell if it's confidence or arrogance.

Even though I'm still recovering from a breakup, I can't say I'd turn down a night to be in his arms. The thought of him talking dirty to me has my panties wet.

I'm sure he uses these smooth lines on dozens of women. I guess you could say Matthew turned me off from men in general.

"I'm not looking to be added to your long list of conquests. Thank you, though." I brush my hands over the front of my skirt, fixing my jacket.

Cody is behind me, kneeling on the floor helping pick up what's left of the refreshments now littering the ground.

Mr. Dreamy's eyes roam over my body and down to my feet before peering back up to meet mine again.

"Why? Or is it because your friend already called dibs?" He quirks his brow.

My cheeks flame again, sending a warning glance over at Cody, who pushes himself to stand. Cody presses his lips together, trying to hold back whatever he's thinking. Mr. Dreamy barks out a laugh, shaking his head at the two of us.

I grit my teeth, ready to get away from both of them.

The PA system buzzes, and Carter's voice filters through the speakers.

"Ladies and gentlemen, this is your pilot speaking. Sadly, due to the winter storm hitting the east coast, all flights out of JFK have been canceled. The high winds and low visibility have made it too risky for us to fly. I'm sorry for the disappointment. I hope to have you fly with us once the weather clears. Please wait for further instruction before deplaning."

"Damnit," I mutter.

"Looks like we're stuck here for another night," Dreamy adds.

Cody nods for me to follow him and we both make our way toward the front of the plane.

"I had a feeling this was going to happen," I whisper to Cody.

It wouldn't be so bad being stuck here if the weather didn't make it impossible to leave to do anything fun. I'll be stranded in my hotel room for the night, which I guess is a good thing considering I have homework to do. Thankfully, for reasons like this, I always bring my laptop with me.

"Well, at least you're stuck here with me." He grins. "We can have a girl's night in with movies, wine, and room service."

He bites his lower lip to smother his grin.

"Oh Lord, do I even want to know?"

He turns his back to face the passengers so only I can see him. He lifts his hand in the air, swiveling his hips in the process, dancing provocatively.

"If you're out here speaking to the Lord, no, you won't want to know. You'll be disappointed in me and all my sins." He cackles and I smack him on the chest.

I do a quick sweep of the passengers before my eyes land on Mr. Dreamy. He flashes me a wink and I bite the corner of my mouth to resist the urge to grin.

The thoughts running through my mind are downright sinful.

I guess that makes two of us.

CHAPTER FOUR

EMMY

We make it back to the Radisson JFK without any issues. I'm ready for a nap by the time we get checked into our room. Cody is gone when I wake up, so I decide to sneak down to the restaurant in search of something to eat.

I don't want to spend the evening alone in my room, so I pack up my laptop and bring it with me, claiming a booth in the corner. I fire off a text message to Cody, asking him where the hell he's at before demanding he meet me for dinner.

I have my head buried in schoolwork when I hear a low whistle from across the room. My head jolts up to find Cody strutting toward me.

"Hey, boo." He blows me a kiss, sliding into the booth seat across from me.

"Where have you been?"

"Don't worry about it. I had some business I needed to attend to."

I raise my brow. "What sort of business?"

He grins. "Oh, you know. A little of this, a little of that."

I shake my head. "Who is it?"

He pulls out his lip gloss, unscrewing the cap, and drags some along his lips. He blots them together, puckering them to blow me a kiss before tucking it back into his pocket.

"Please don't tell me you're seeing Evan again. It's him, isn't it?"

"I don't know what you're talking about." He snickers.

It's him. I know it's him by the mock expression of innocence on his face.

Evan is a pilot for another airline. They've been hooking up off and on for over six months. I've seen him a few times, but don't know much about him.

From what I've gathered in the past, he likes to keep his relationships private. I don't blame him, but Cody isn't the type of person to be kept hidden.

I've tried asking Cody about it before, but he always insists it's just for fun. The fact they've been seeing each other for so long has me wondering if there's more to it.

I just don't want to see my friend hurt in the way I was by Matthew.

"Are you two getting serious, or what is this exactly?"

"I'm single like a Pringle, baby." He snaps his fingers and tilts his head to the side. "I like to keep my options open. Until someone's ready to name me and claim me, I won't be taking this off the market."

He waves his hand, accentuating his curves, and I giggle.

"There's nothing wrong with exploring what's on the menu, baby girl. Now that you're on the market, you should be doing the same. You need to get out and explore, taste what is out there before you settle down with one person."

I've been in three serious relationships since I was in high school. Even between relationships, I was never the type to date around. If I'm interested in someone, I'm investing all my time and energy into them and not looking elsewhere.

Call me a hopeless romantic, but it's how I've always been.

"I'm not the type of girl who can hook up," I say, honestly.

"Don't think of it as hooking up. You need to put yourself out there and live your life. Honey, you are only twenty-two years old. You have no business settling down right now."

He's right. I've been too focused on my relationship with Matthew for the last two years.

Why was I so willing to waste my time on a man who wasn't putting in the same effort that I was?

I'm young, though, and you only get to live these years once. Might as well make them worth it.

"I'm not the type to see more than one person, though. Don't you think that could get messy?"

"I think you shouldn't put all your eggs in one basket. Some men think with the wrong head and are always horny. Hell, I had one sexting me while I was in the middle of Whole Foods. I played along until he asked me to send nudes."

He rolls his eyes and curls his lip. "I was standing there, holding a damn eggplant while he was asking if I was turned on."

I bark out a laugh, slapping my hand over my mouth, trying to contain myself, picturing him standing there.

I notice Mr. Dreamy stroll into the restaurant toward the bar, quickly silencing me in the process. His eyes do a slow sweep of the room before landing on me.

I suck in a breath at the sight of his smoldering stare, noticing the subtle tick in his jaw. His eyes flash down to my mouth before meeting my gaze once more.

"Of course, he's staying here," I whisper to Cody while never taking my eyes off him.

He claims a spot at the end of the bar, closest to us, giving him a direct shot to my line of sight.

My eyes drag over his tall frame, down to the black sweatshirt and sweatpants he's wearing, with a pair of white sneakers. He's dressed down, a complete opposite of the man at the airport, wearing his fitted suit and tie.

His hair looks damp, like he just got out of the shower and ran a towel through it, not bothering to style it before he came down in search of something to eat.

Cody glances over his shoulder to look at him before turning back to face me.

"I told you to go live your life. Wild and free, remember?" He grins, reaching across the table to grab my hand.

The waitress comes over and I'm grateful for the distraction, not wanting to have this conversation right now. In fact, I think I'm ready to put my homework away for the night and indulge a little.

"I'll take a strawberry margarita. On the rocks, please. The biggest one you got."

"Okay, girlfriend. Okay," Cody sings. "I'll have what she's having, please."

I haven't eaten much, so I settle on a buffalo chicken wrap, knowing if I don't get something in my stomach, I'll end up two sheets to the wind quicker than I would've intended.

The last thing I need is to oversleep again tomorrow.

Our flight got rescheduled, so I need to be awake and ready to go, or it'll make for another long day.

My phone dings with a notification, so I swipe to check the screen and notice an email came through from Michael Jacobs.

My heart rate spikes as my eyes scan over the screen, landing on the word congratulations. My hand slaps over my mouth, and my eyes widen.

"Oh my God, what?" Cody screeches.

"I got the internship." I drop my phone, staring up at him. "I frickin' got the internship. Can you believe it?"

"I knew you would." He claps.

He slides out of the seat and rounds the table, wrapping his arms around me in a big hug, swaying us from side to side.

"I'm so proud of you."

My eyes meet Dreamy's across the bar over Cody's shoulder, and he flashes me a wink.

I'm grinning when Cody pulls back and grips my face in his hands, then smacks a big kiss on my cheek.

"My girl is going to be the next big fashion designer, everyone. Watch out! Before too long, you'll be maxing out them credit cards wearing all her beautiful clothes."

I'm beaming, unable to contain my happiness. I don't know where I'd be without Cody. He's always been my biggest supporter since we met three years ago.

I'm glad that while taking the internship I'll only be moving away from him for the summer. Plus, it's not like we won't see each other when I'm working for the airline. I don't know what I'd do without him.

It's one thing to have moved away from my parents when I graduated, but it's another thing to find friends who become like family. Cody's like a brother to me.

"This calls for a celebration." He claps. He looks over to the waitress behind the bar, holding his hand up in the air. "Can we get a round of shots, too, while you're at it?"

I laugh. "This could be trouble."

"The best kind of trouble involves bad decisions. It'll be okay."

Dreamy holds his hand up, nodding toward the two of us. I watch as the waitress adds a third glass to the lineup.

She sets one shot in front of him before she rounds the bar, bringing the other two and our margaritas to us.

"This round is on Mr. Wild." She signals over to him.

Mr. Wild?

His name rolled around in my head, mixing with Cody's comment earlier about living life wild and free.

He raises his shot glass up to us in cheers, and I smile at him before tipping my head back and tossing the shot down. The liquor burns my throat, and I grit my teeth, letting it warm my cheeks.

Cody picks up his phone and begins to furiously type away.

"Evan wants me to come by his room later," he says. "You won't be mad, will you?"

"Why would I be?"

"Well, we're having our movie night tonight, remember?"

"I don't mind. I'll probably end up dragging my ass upstairs and will fall asleep watching an old episode of *Friends*."

"You're so predictable."

I shrug.

"You know, you could always find something else to do. Or should I say, someone else?"

He nods his head toward Wild and Dreamy. Heat blazes over my face and I flash my eyes in his direction, wondering if he's heard Cody talking about him again.

I notice the subtle tick in his jaw is back before his eyes glance over to meet mine.

I change the subject entirely, bringing up the internship and plans for the summer. By the time Cody finishes his margarita and I've eaten dinner, I'm halfway through my drink and feeling the buzz zipping through me as the effects start to run their course.

Cody sighs, relaxing against the booth seat. "I'm ready to go see my man now."

I giggle, covering my mouth when it comes out louder than I expected.

"The things I'd let that man do to me." He waves his hand and shakes his head. "He could bang me like a screen door in a hurricane."

I snort, sending us both into a fit of laughter.

Cody offers to walk me up to our room, but I wave him off, insisting I'll be fine on my own. I take a few more sips of my margarita before telling myself I'm done. I'm not drunk by any means, but I'm feelin' it now.

I scroll through social media on my phone for a bit before packing up my laptop bag.

"Is this seat still taken?" His deep voice causes my body to tremble as I slowly drag my eyes over his body.

"No, he took off. It's just me now."

"I was hoping I'd get a chance to have you alone," he mutters low.

"Why is that exactly? I would've thought after our run in today, both times, you'd want to stay far away from me."

He nods. "I owe you an apology. I think we got off on the wrong foot. I made assumptions about you and why you bumped into me."

My brows furrow. "What were your assumptions of me exactly?"

He ducks his head. "It's going to sound cocky, but I don't mean for it to be. I'm used to women throwing themselves at me for selfish reasons. I knew the second you fired off that mouth of yours, though, I was wrong about you."

I want to press him on it more. There's something about it that tells me this isn't the time or place, though. Not to mention, I want to take Cody's advice about living and having fun. A conversation about him with other women doesn't fit into that category at all.

"I think we were both wrong about each other." I smile, reaching for my glass of water, and take a sip. "Thanks for the drinks earlier, too, by the way." I set the glass down, brushing my fingers through the condensation, letting it cool my skin.

"I'm glad we both ended up here tonight, and I have the chance to get to know the real you."

CHAPTER FIVE

JAXSEN

There's something about the fact she has no idea who I am that makes me even more attracted to her.

It's refreshing and freeing, and something about it makes me want to spend more time with her.

"You got a new job, huh?" I ask.

Her dark hair is piled on top of her head in one of those messy buns, with strands of hair pulled down, framing her face. She doesn't have an ounce of makeup on and is dressed down in an oversized sweater.

She has a light dust of freckles on the apples of her cheeks and nose. She's wearing a pair of dark-framed glasses. The sight of her like this is different than the woman I saw today, and a stark contrast to the women I've dated in the past.

Hell, the last girl I was seeing for over six months wouldn't let me see her without makeup. She woke up before me every morning and immediately escaped to the bathroom where she'd shower and do her makeup, all before she had a chance to sit down and eat breakfast.

"It's an internship. I'm from Chicago, studying fashion design right now."

She takes another sip of water before reaching for her laptop bag and lifts the strap over her head.

We're both here, away from home. After the storm passes, she'll make her way back home to Chicago, and I'll head back to Miami. Although I visit Chicago from time to time for games, I know we'll likely never see each other again.

She doesn't have the slightest clue who I am, which means she probably won't be hitting up any Miami Blaze games any time soon.

"Can I walk you to your room?"

Her cheeks turn rosy. My fingers itch to reach across the table and brush my thumb over her soft skin. She nods, sliding out of the booth seat.

I do the same, brushing my hand against hers when I offer to take her bag. She stares up at me beneath her long lashes, assuring me it's okay.

I follow along behind her out of the restaurant and through the lobby, over to the bay of elevators.

"What floor are you on?" she asks.

Her eyes remain fixated on my mouth, waiting for me to answer, and her tongue slides out as it brushes across her lower lip.

"Eight."

"I'm on six." She smiles.

I reach around her to press the button for the elevator, molding my chest against her back. The urge to drag her into the elevator and kiss her consumes me. I want to forget everything about what happened today before meeting her. Now that it's on my mind, it's impossible to think about anything else.

When the elevator dings, I press my hand against the small of her back and lead her inside. She leans against the wall across from me, her hands gripping the railing behind her.

The sexual tension between us is mounting. The moment the door closes, I throw all caution to the wind and take the two steps separating us. She winces when she drops her bag on the floor with a loud thud. My hands press against the side of her face, tilting her chin up toward me.

The elevator beeps as we pass each floor. Without thinking, I reach my hand out and hit the stop button forcing the elevator to lurch to a halt.

"I need you alone." I grin, while brushing her hair away from her face. I run my thumb over her cheek. When she slowly drags her tongue across her lower lip, I give in, and my lips crash down on hers.

She releases a throaty moan. Her fingers grip the front of my sweatshirt, holding me against her. She slides her arms up, wrapping them around my neck, holding on for the ride.

I break the kiss moving to nip and bite along her collarbone and up her neck.

"Oh God," she moans.

"Hello, is everything all right?" A voice filters through the speaker, and she sucks in a breath, bringing us back to reality.

"Uhh, yeah," I mutter, clearing my throat.

I reach over to hit the stop button, causing the elevator to bounce. I press my hands against the wall, caging her in, keeping us both steady on our feet. Lord knows, having my mouth on her has me feeling weak as it is.

"Thanks for checking," I say, noticing the red light on the intercom is still on. We start to move again. When the light shuts off, I shift my gaze back to her.

Her arms are crossed over her chest, her hand over her mouth, rubbing her thumb along her lips to try and conceal her smile.

The elevator stops on the sixth floor. I know I should step back, but I'm not ready to leave her. Not yet.

"Come to my room," I whisper.

She looks back at me, appearing to consider it for a moment. She whispers something under her breath that sounds like, "Live a little." I don't know if she realizes she said it out loud before nodding, letting the door slide shut.

I link our fingers together, and she bends down to pick up her bag. She lifts the strap over her shoulder before the elevator dings, announcing we've made it to the eighth floor.

I'm thankful my room isn't too far because I don't want to wait another second to get her alone.

She giggles watching me fumble with my wallet, pulling out my room key before sliding it into the lock. Shoving the door open, I reach for her hand and pull her inside with me.

Her mouth curves into a sweet smile when I lift her into my arms. She slips her arms around my neck before her mouth crashes down on mine.

"Fuck," I moan.

Her legs wrap around my waist, and I'm grateful she's dressed in a pair of thin leggings, letting me feel the heat of her pussy when she grinds against me.

She drags her nails through my hair, and I turn to carry her into the room, setting her on top of the long dresser at the foot of the bed.

There's a bed right behind us, but where's the fun in that?

I pull back, lifting my sweatshirt over my head, and toss it on top of my suitcase.

Desire glosses over her eyes when she sees the tattoo spanning across my chest and arms. She follows along, removing her glasses, folding them, and sitting them next to her on the dresser. She shrugs out of her sweater before lifting the hem of the tank top underneath, tossing them on top of mine.

Drinking in every inch of her body, my hands roam over her smooth skin and curves. What makes her even sexier is she doesn't even move to cover herself, not like most women I've been with do. Even with the lights on and my eyes on her, she doesn't pull away from me.

"Take your hair down."

She smiles, reaching her hand up to untie it, letting her long dark brown hair fall in waves around her. She reaches between her breasts, unhooking her bra. She lowers the straps and lets it drop to the floor beneath us.

The sight of her pert nipples, soft pink against her tan skin, has my mouth watering to taste her.

"You ..." My voice trails off. "You are fuckin' beautiful."

Her cheeks flush again. I love seeing how her body reacts to me, and the thought has me eager to find all the other ways I can inflict the same response.

I skate my hands over her thick thighs, up toward the band of her leggings, and pull them down her legs.

She spreads them open for me, completely naked now. She wasn't wearing any panties. Something about the thought makes it hard for me to swallow.

"Shit," I mutter to myself.

She reaches her hand out toward me, cupping me over the front of my sweatpants before she dips her hand inside, gripping my dick.

"Motherfucker," I roll my head back, squeezing my eyes shut.

She fists my dick in her small hand. I eagerly reach down to untie the drawstring of my sweats and push them over my hips. I stare down at her, watching as she adjusts her grip, dragging her tongue over her lower lip. When she swipes her thumb over the tip, I know I won't last long.

"I want to be inside you when I cum," I moan, staring down to where her hand strokes me slowly.

I lick my finger and reach between her legs, brushing my thumb over her swollen clit. She reclines back and lets her trembling legs fall open.

I squeeze my dick, attempting to fight off my release.

She runs her hands over her stomach, up toward her breasts, tweaking her nipple. The sight of her turned on, touching herself while she watches me is too fuckin' much.

My fingers dig into her hips, lifting her closer to the edge of the dresser. I bend down and trace my tongue along her pussy lips before slowly flicking her clit.

She releases a throaty moan. Her body shudders as I adjust her legs over my shoulders.

The sounds she makes mixed with the taste of her sweetness have me wanting to stay here all night. I wasn't lying, though; I want to be inside her when we cum.

I'm confident, I won't last long once I slide into her tight pussy if I continue.

Brushing the tip of my dick through her wet folds, I pull back and stand, needing to find my wallet to grab a condom.

"I'm clean," she mutters. I'm almost surprised by the comment, given we just met. "I've only been with two men. My last boyfriend cheated on me. I got tested after that. I'm on birth control, too, and I'm clean."

I grip her face in my hands, my mouth crashing down on hers in a soul-searing kiss.

When I pull back, I rub the tip of my dick over her clit, and her head falls back, her eyes screwing shut.

"I'm clean too," I whisper, just as I push inside her.

A thought drifts into the back of my mind telling me this is reckless and irresponsible, but I don't care. I hardly know anything about her, yet here I am, sharing something so intimate and personal.

Yet, I feel like I can trust her too.

This feels more intense and real than any other time before, and I barely even know her.

When her arms wrap around my neck and she kisses me again, I thrust my hips hard, burying myself inside her.

I'm in deep, so deep I don't even want to come up for air.

It's wild and reckless, and even if it's only for tonight, she is mine.

CHAPTER SIX

JAXSEN

"Shit, suck, fuck, motherfuck."

The grunts and moans that follow have me peeking my eyes open before squeezing them shut, fighting against the sunlight shining through the window, nearly blinding me.

The mattress moves near my feet, and it dawns on me someone's in the room before memories from the night before come flooding back.

Dark hair, honey-colored eyes, and those curves made for sin. Her smooth skin and her breathtaking smile are all I can see.

When I slowly blink my eyes open again, she is standing at the foot of the bed, bent over at the waist with her round ass pointed at me while she stumbles trying to pull on her leggings.

My mouth goes dry, and I swipe my tongue over my lower lip at the sight of her. She must hear me suck in a breath when her eyes shoot over to look at me.

"Uhh, hi." She forces a smile, pulling her pants over her butt. She snatches her shirt off the floor, using it to cover her chest.

Ahh, now she's trying to be modest when she didn't seem to care one bit last night.

"Good morning." A slow smile stretches over my face, as memories from the night before begin swirling around in my mind.

After our first time on the dresser, we went again on the bed before our last round in the shower. I spent some time between her legs before she came again, passing out after I made her cum for the fourth time.

My body aches, my arms are sore. I was spent in the most glorious way possible.

"Give me a minute, and I'll be out of your hair." She smiles.

Out of my hair? Is she serious?

"Or you could stay …"

She shakes her head and smiles. "We had enough fun last night. I need to hurry, or I'm going to be late for work."

I push myself up, swinging my legs over the side of the bed. I'm still naked, the sheet draped over my lower body.

I glance over at her when she clears her throat, just before she tosses my underwear at me, nearly hitting me in the face. I reach up and snatch them, slipping them on before I stand.

She meets my eyes in the mirror, pulling her long hair back on top of her head. I want to run my hands through the soft strands again.

Who the hell am I?

Since when have I ever thought about touching a woman in ways she has me fantasizing about touching her?

When she sees me sauntering toward her, she turns and starts to back away, holding her hand out to stop me.

"What?" I grin. "Why are you running away from me now?"

"Listen ..." She trails off, and I chuckle.

"Jaxsen."

"Jaxsen," she repeats, seeming to consider my name before she continues. "Listen, Jaxsen, last night was great. Amazing. Wonderful. It truly was."

"Great ..." I trail off.

"Emmy," she follows up, which reminds me of the day before, when her friend announced their name on the plane. He called her Emerson.

"Great, Emmy. Why does it have to stop there?"

She drops her hand, her eyes widening as if telling me she's serious and to drop the playful act.

"It has to stop here before, well, 'cause I have to get ready for work, and you have a flight to catch. And because this was supposed to be one night of fun, with no intention of it becoming more."

"It doesn't have to be only one night, though. Even though we both need to leave, maybe I can see you the next time I'm in Chicago?"

"I'm not looking for anything serious. I just got out of a relationship not too long ago."

"Right, I remember. Sad dick balloons. Got it," I joke.

She throws her head back and laughs. It's the type of laugh that hits you unexpectedly and you're clutching your stomach trying to keep it together.

Her phone vibrates on the dresser, and she quickly swipes it before muttering, "Shit," under her breath.

"I'm sorry, I really do have to get going, or I'm going to make the rest of the crew late."

I check the time on the alarm clock sitting on the nightstand and realize I don't have much time myself if I want to get cleaned up before my car arrives to take me to the airport.

She pulls her sweater on, taking a quick glance in the mirror to check her appearance.

"It was great to meet you."

"Can I at least get your number?" I ask, blurting it out as she turns to walk toward the door, grabbing her laptop bag from where I hung it up the night before.

She pulls the strap over her shoulder and turns back toward me, considering it for a moment. She rakes her teeth over her lower lip before she nods, holding her hand out for my phone.

I quickly rush to the side of the bed, swiping my phone off the floor from where it fell, and hand it over to her.

Her tense expression relaxes and she types in her number. When she goes to pass the phone back, I brush my hand over the back of hers, and her cheeks warm again.

As much as she wants to play it off like it was one night, I sense from the way her body reacts to me, she feels the connection between us too.

Pulling her toward me, I press a kiss against her cheek. When I pull back, she flashes me a warm smile and whispers, "Thank you."

"Bye Emmy," I murmur.

"Bye Jaxsen," she replies, reaching behind her back to grab the door handle.

When the door shuts behind her, I run my hand over the back of the door. There's an unsettling feeling inside me telling me this is the last time I'll ever see her, and I hate to think it's true.

We've already had our last game of the season in Chicago. Unless we happen to meet them in the playoffs, it could be a while before I'm back there again.

I check my messages and see a text from Candyce, my assistant, reminding me when my car will be arriving. I only have twenty minutes if I have any hope of making it on time. I quickly jump in the shower to clean myself up before throwing on the sweatshirt and joggers from the night before.

I hadn't planned on staying in the city for another night, so I'm running low on clothing options. The last thing I wanted was to wear my suit to the airport again.

I don't mind getting dressed up from time to time, but I prefer wearing something comfortable. My gym shorts and a T-shirt are my go-to when I'm home.

When I make it to the airport an hour later and board my flight, I keep my eyes peeled for any sight of Emmy. I spot her friend, Cody, from the night before. It takes him a second to recognize me with my hat pulled low. I see a flash of recognition hit him, and he winks when he realizes it's me.

I nod in greeting. I'm curious if he happened to hear about our time together or if he's simply thinking about last night at the bar.

Anytime I've flown commercial, I've always made it a point to have Candyce book me a seat in first class. I'm used to being in the public eye, it comes with the territory, but with the media hot on my ass lately, I'm trying to fly under the radar as much as possible.

When the pre-flight announcements kickoff and I don't see Emmy anywhere, I start to wonder if she made it on time.

I reach into my pocket and shoot off a message to her.

Me: Hey, it's Jaxsen. I hope you made it on time for work this morning. I had a good time last night and I meant what I said about hoping to see you again. Hit me up if you find yourself in Miami. I'll do the same when I get back to Chicago. Drinks on me.

When Cody passes by a few minutes later, holding out a bottle of water, I nod and take it from him.

"I hope Emmy wasn't late this morning," I say, and immediately feel bad for bringing it up, not wanting to get into her business.

"Why would you be worried about Emmy being late this morning?" He emphasizes the end, and I realize there's a chance he has no idea she stayed with me.

Shit.

"I, uh, saw her this morning when she went to get breakfast. She mentioned she left her key in her room and was worried she'd be late for work."

His eyes narrow, not sure if he wants to believe me or not. I flash him a small smile, and his mouth curves in a smirk, shaking his head.

"How sweet of you to worry about her," he retorts. "She ended up swapping with someone and is covering coach for this trip."

I nod, sitting back against the seat. I twist the cap to my water and take a swig, muttering a low, "Thanks."

Music starts to play overhead. I recognize the song from the day before but can't remember the name to save my life. It's been years since I've heard it.

I turn my phone on airplane mode and shove my earbuds in, deciding to listen to music and get some shut-eye on the flight home. I wake halfway through and stare out the window, taking in the sights of the clouds below us.

As much as I enjoyed the night with Emmy, the distraction got my mind off the shitstorm waiting for me in Miami; I know I can't keep reality away for too long.

The meeting with the commissioner and the league's big wigs is behind me. When I get home, something is going to have to change. Especially if I have any hope or chance of getting my team to the finals.

If I don't get it together, I risk blowing the entire season. Not to mention my career, all in the blink of an eye.

I know there are teams out there who would want me, even if Miami releases me when my contract is up this fall, but I spent my whole career playing for the Blaze. I don't want to leave the team, coaches, or fans who have supported me this far.

The last twenty-four hours have felt like an escape for me. Once the wheels hit the runway and I'm back in Miami, it's back to the real world again.

I dread turning my phone back on, appreciating the much-needed reprieve. I've always been one to avoid social media and the news, especially with all the speculation over my future with the league.

A flood of text messages and emails hit my notifications, but I ignore all of them, scrolling until I see a message ping come through from Emmy.

A grin curves my mouth. I glance around me, searching for any sign of her.

The thought of her being on the flight, within reach, has me silently wishing I could convince her to stay in Miami for the night with me.

Emmy: Emmy?

Emmy: Sorry, bud, hate to break it to ya but she gave you the wrong number. This is Matthew, her ex.

I drag my hand over my chin and shake my head, feeling the facial hair prick my skin.

She gave me the wrong fuckin' number.

Matter of fact, she gave me her ex's number.

Sad dick balloons.

I'll be damned. I don't recall the last time I was rejected by someone, much less by a girl who has no idea who the hell I am.

Guess there's a first time for everything.

CHAPTER SEVEN

EMMY
SIX WEEKS LATER

"We have a full schedule this week. Mostly clients coming in for fittings. It's important to be on your game, as many are Michael Jacobs's best customers," Kaylee croons.

I follow along behind her down the narrow hallway to the front of the boutique.

Shortly after I landed the internship, I flew into Miami for a few days to meet with Jillian, the director. We got together for lunch, and I was introduced to the rest of the team along with the two other girls who got internships with me. While I was there, I made a point to try and figure out my living situation.

What made it difficult was knowing I only planned to stay for the summer. I was on a limited budget, which made finding a place even more challenging.

Kaylee has worked with Jillian for a couple years now. As soon as I brought up how I was looking for a place to stay, she jumped on board and said she's been looking for a roommate. We hit it off immediately, and she's quickly become a close friend of mine.

I missed being home with my friends, close to my family, but I loved being in the warm weather. It's hard to be sad and homesick when you have the Florida sun shining on you every day.

"I'll have you answering the phones and greeting guests when they walk in. We'll work together through fittings. If there are any adjustments, we'll need to make arrangements right away, as our appointments are booking quickly."

I nod, soaking in every detail. It's my second week and I've already learned so much.

I knew it was going to be a challenge balancing the internship and my job at the airline, especially when both consist of long days. I've been feeling exhausted, but I keep reminding myself it's for my dream.

I am not going to take this opportunity for granted. If I'm tired, I'll be tired. I'll sleep when I'm dead.

I immediately get busy organizing a row of suits for fittings, sorting them by arrival time, when the doorbell rings. I turn toward the door, ready to greet our first client of the morning, when my eyes meet a familiar pair of crystal blues. My mouth drops open, nearly hitting the floor.

His eyes widen in recognition before a slow smile stretches across his face. Everything seems to move in slow motion from there.

I attempt to snap myself out of it, forcing my feet to move. I can't ignore the sound of my own heartbeat in my ears, practically beating out of my damn chest.

"Well, hello, Emmy. It's good to see you again, here in Miami, no less. It is Emmy, right?" he questions.

I move to the long desk toward the front of the boutique, ready to check him in, when my hands pause, and I narrow my eyes on him.

"It may be hard for you to remember, but yes. My name is, in fact, Emmy."

When I met him back in New York, I knew he was the type who had women throwing themselves at him, leaving a long list of conquests in his wake. He confirmed it with one simple question.

"I guess I can't be certain. You lied about your number. It appears you lied about living in Chicago. Who knows what else you lied to me about? What an interesting turn of events though, to find you here in Miami."

I swallow hard at the mention of giving him the wrong number. I blocked Matthew after he kept calling me incessantly. I never stopped to consider if it was because Jaxsen contacted him in hopes of reaching me.

I can't help but wonder how the conversation went and what led him to finding out it was, in fact, not my number.

I press my lips together to hold back the smile that threatens to break across my face. He must notice it, his eyes narrowing, and he shakes his head.

"Listen, I'm sorry." I glance around me, not wanting anyone to overhear our conversation. "I shouldn't have given you the wrong number. It's rude, and I certainly didn't mean to offend you. At the time, I had just gone through a very bad breakup, and I wasn't ready for more and—"

He holds his hand up. "You were going through a breakup and weren't interested in anything more beyond one night. I get it. I've been there myself."

I nod. He flashes me an understanding smile. "It's okay."

"Do you have an appointment?" I ask, attempting to change the subject.

"A fitting scheduled for ten."

I check the appointments and see the name Candyce Hendrix listed at our ten o'clock spot. My mind flips into overdrive, wondering who Candyce could be.

Does he have a girlfriend? Were they together when we hooked up too?

My stomach rolls at the thought of being the other woman after everything that happened with Matthew.

"Well, look who it is. Mr. Jaxsen Wild." Kaylee struts out of the backroom, a devious smirk on her face.

I flash a nervous smile at him before my gaze bounces to Kaylee, wondering if there's a history between the two of them.

Wait, did she just say Jaxsen Wild? Why does that name sound familiar?

Kaylee is dressed in a pair of black trouser shorts and a white sleeveless peplum top. Black earrings dangle from her ears and her signature megawatt smile earns one of Jaxsen's heart-stopping grins in return.

They are definitely friendly with each other, and the thought causes my stomach to flip.

I bite down on my bottom lip, attempting to cover the annoyance causing my blood to simmer.

The worst part is I know I have no reason to feel jealous, but that's what I'm feeling. Red, hot jealousy.

Out of all the places in the world, I never expected to run into him here.

"Hey Kaylee," he smirks.

"You think you got this season in the bag?" She quirks her brow. "I've been watching, cheering you on."

Jaxsen straightens his back, his eyes flit over to mine. He nods and replies with a thank you.

"You remember Jaxsen, don't you?" Kaylee asks, glancing over at me, changing the subject.

My eyes widen and my body tenses. "I don't think so ..." I mumble, dragging the words out.

Why does the name sound so familiar?

I have no idea how to respond, especially with his gaze burning into me.

"Jaxsen is the point guard for the Miami Blaze."

It dawns on me then where the name sounds familiar. Kaylee has talked about watching the Miami Blaze play in the playoffs all week. One of her best friends, Sydney, is dating another player on the team, Colson Rush.

Memories of the first time I saw Jaxsen at the airport roll through my mind, recalling how several passengers on the plane were whispering and pointing in his direction. He kept his head down and his sunglasses on, trying to avoid any attention.

There's no way Jaxsen's oblivious to how attractive he is. I bet he has women tripping over themselves for a night with him like I had back in the city. Yet, here I was, giving him my ex's phone number.

"I can take Jaxsen off your hands if you want to continue getting organized for our appointments today," Kaylee suggests, smiling at me before fluttering her eyelashes back at him.

The knot coiling in my stomach tightens. I hate how it bothers me when I have no justifiable reason. Especially after the way I left and treated him.

I shouldn't care if Kaylee is interested, or what sort of history they have together.

"Sure thing." I smile, stepping back from the counter.

"Actually, if you don't mind, I was hoping to catch up with Emmy for a bit. Old friends. I haven't had a chance to talk to her for a while."

Old friends? I just told her I didn't know who he was and he's claiming we're *old friends.*

"Is that right?" Kaylee sneers. She flashes Jaxsen a wink. "I guess I'll leave you to it."

I roll my lips together, avoiding the heat from Kaylee's questioning stare burning into the side of my face.

There will be no escaping her questions later. Eventually, I'll have to come clean about our history, but now isn't the time or the place to do it. Especially with him standing a foot in front of me, reminding me of the last time I saw him and how delicious he looked with nothing but the white sheet around his waist.

Don't think about it, Emmy. Don't even think about it.

I release a slow breath once the two of us are finally alone. I turn my attention back to the computer.

"I don't see an appointment in our system under your name."

"Try the name Candyce Hendrix."

I nod. He must sense the questions swirling through my mind when he follows it up with, "Candyce is my assistant, not my girlfriend."

I shrug. "It's not my business, Jaxsen."

He narrows his eyes, the blue depths piercing into my soul with one look. I notice the subtle tick of his jaw.

He slips his hands into his pockets and rocks on the soles of his feet.

"I'll be right back. Let me grab the suit for you. I'll meet you in the front near the dressing rooms." I point toward the area closed off with a row of three fitting rooms, each one with a cognac wooden door.

A tan leather couch with two chairs is positioned in front of them, with a coffee table in the middle and a large gold chandelier hanging overhead.

Jaxsen looks so out of place here, dressed in his red athletic shorts, black T-shirt, and black sneakers. He looks every bit of the basketball player I now know him to be and nothing like the CEO I pegged him for when we first met.

He's a mirage of walking contradictions.

I step into the backroom to the row of suits hanging in garment bags. I spot the one with his name printed in large black letters and carry it with me toward the front.

Jaxsen is seated in one of the chairs, facing a mirror. He spots me walking toward him in our reflection, his eyes tracking me across the room. He slowly drags his eyes down my body, to my legs, and back up to my face by the time I reach him.

He moves to stand, towering over me. His mood has changed now that it's the two of us, reminding me of the cold and stoic man I met back in New York.

He reaches out for the garment bag and his hand brushes over mine, causing my body to tense.

"Do I make you nervous?" His voice is low, deep, and it sends shivers through me.

I shake my head. "You're just hard for me to read sometimes."

"Good."

I furrow my brows.

"I don't need you knowing how I'm picturing dragging you into the fitting room with me and pushing you against the wall again."

My breath hitches, my heart beating wildly at the visual he put into my mind. For a moment, I almost forget where I am and want to taunt him by urging him to do it.

Six weeks ago, I was heartbroken over the way my relationship ended. I wasn't in a place to be pursuing anything, especially with someone as closed off as him.

Jaxsen has heartbreaker written all over him.

He takes a step toward me, eliminating the distance between us. My heart hammers in my chest. I reach my hand up and run my fingers over my skin, damp with a sheen of perspiration.

He leans forward, tilting his head near my ear and whispers, "Do you like the sound of that, Emmy?"

My breath grows heavy, unable to focus on holding myself together. He nips at my earlobe and a muffled moan slips out before my hand darts out to grip his forearm, attempting to steady myself.

I'm putty in his hands, and he knows it.

"I would say that's a yes, wouldn't you?" He hums in appreciation.

I release a slow breath and tilt my head back to look at him, at a loss for words when my eyes lock on his. I nod and tighten my hand holding his arm, my nails digging into his skin.

"Keep it up, and I'll have you digging those nails into my back in less than ten seconds."

I drag my tongue across my lips, wetting them. They're dry from the force of my heavy panting, trying to hold it together.

"I can only imagine how wet you are for me right now." His lids grow heavy, dragging his teeth over his lower lip.

This man could dirty talk the panties right off me.

"Is everything okay?" Kaylee's voice filters across the room. I jump away from Jaxsen like my hand is about to light on fire from touching him.

Jaxsen lifts the garment bag and nods, a slow grin stretching across his face. I force a fake smile and nervously run my hand through my hair, curled down my back.

"Yep," I snap. "We're great. Right, Jaxsen? You should get in there and try your suit on. I can't wait to see how it looks on you."

I rattle the words off and Jaxsen chuckles under his breath.

I chance a glance at Kaylee once the door to the dressing room shuts behind him. She's standing at the counter, her arms folded in front of her, with her brow quirked. The look on her face says, "You're going to explain every last detail to me tonight."

I shake my head, trying to pull myself together, remembering I'm working. I have no business letting a man like him distract me, here of all places.

When my eyes meet my reflection in the mirror once more, I notice the glow highlighting my skin, and I bite my lip to avoid smiling.

Yeah. I'd let Jaxsen wreck my world any day.

CHAPTER EIGHT

EMMY

"Please don't tell me you're going to stay in all night like a lame ass," Kaylee chirps, poking her head into my bedroom.

As soon as I got home, I didn't waste any time shedding my heels and clothes, swapping them out for a pair of leggings and a tank top.

Tomorrow I am back on the road for my weekend shift with the airline. In the meantime, I need to try and tackle as much homework as I can.

"I'm not a lame ass." I scoff. "I have homework to do. Something you should probably do too."

Kaylee landed a job at Michael Jacobs after her internship with them last year. Sometimes I'm envious of how she has more free time to enjoy the summer. While I'm bouncing between jobs or shoving my head into my books, she's off hitting the beach, a club, or like tonight, a game.

"You deserve one night off. You haven't done anything all week but work, work out, or do homework. You're too young to have no social life. It's too much work and not enough play."

I slouch against my headboard, crossing my arms over my head. I already took my makeup off, and my hair is tied up in a knot. I'm nowhere near ready to go anywhere, even though the thought of going out does sound fun.

I've been here for going on three weeks and still haven't taken the time to get out and explore.

"What are you doing tonight?"

"Sydney scored us tickets to the Blaze game. She has three tickets, one for me and her, and I told her I'd see if you wanted to come."

Basketball? I don't know anything about basketball, honestly.

"You can't say no. It's the playoffs."

She says that like it's supposed to sway me, yet I still don't have the slightest clue who the Blaze are, aside from the fact Jaxsen plays for them. I wouldn't be able to follow a damn thing happening.

I stare down at the stack of books sprawled out in front of me and glance back up at her. She leans her shoulder against the doorframe, her brows furrowed and her arms crossed. The look on her face says she's not willing to accept no for an answer.

"How much time do I have to get ready?" I ask, releasing a heavy sigh.

"We need to leave here in forty minutes. I'll even let you borrow one of my jerseys so you can fit in with the rest of us."

"Uhm ..." I hold my hand up, stopping her. That wouldn't be necessary.

"You'll be wearing a jersey, Em, and you're gonna have fun. Now get your butt up off the bed and get your ass in gear."

She smirks and I move to climb off the bed. She spins on her heel and disappears down the hallway. She probably went to her closet in search of what she wants me to wear.

I'm envious of all her clothes. Her closet is like every woman's dream. Before too long, she's going to need another bedroom to hold all her stuff.

I escape into the ensuite bathroom and quickly let my hair down, surprised it still managed to hold a curl from how I styled it this morning. I run my fingers through the strands, attempting to make sense of it before I pull out my makeup.

I opt to keep it light, not needing to get all done up for the game. I recently tried out the reverse cat eye, giving my undereye a smoky look. I swipe some light champagne eyeshadow on my eyelid, to avoid looking too dark, and add some mascara and gloss to my lips.

In a matter of twenty minutes, I manage to go from looking ready for bed to ready to take on the Miami nightlife by storm.

Kaylee comes bounding into my room a few minutes later, ready to fight me some more if I'm not ready, when her eyes widen at my face in the mirror.

"Damn, girl." She grins, holding a shirt under her arm.

I turn around and laugh, rubbing my lips together and shaking my head at her antics.

"Here." She tosses me a jersey and I shoot my hand up to catch it before it lands on my face.

There's a crowd of people waiting outside the arena with lines forming through the ticket gate when we arrive forty-five minutes later. Thankfully, we're able to get through quickly with Sydney's connections and get to our seats in the nick of time.

I'm surprised when I find Sydney scored us some pretty decent seats, only the fifth row from the court. We are right behind the players bench on the Miami Blaze side.

"You never did tell me how it went today with Jaxsen," Kaylee mumbles under her breath.

I never told Kaylee about our night together, and I'm not sure if I want to or not. She didn't see what happened between the two of us, but I know she picked up on the tension.

"It's no big deal. I forgot we met once on a flight back from New York. I didn't recognize him, though, until you told me who he was."

I take a swig of my drink, hoping like hell my answer suffices.

"Well, it didn't look like nothing. The way he looks at you is enough to set the whole place on fire."

My eyes dart up, looking around for him. Even with the crowd of people, it's like I can feel his gaze on me, and our eyes immediately lock on each other.

My brows shoot up and a lump forms in my throat, making it difficult to swallow. I take him in, from his tall frame to the black jersey and shorts he's wearing, complete with the bright orange shoes on his feet.

By the time I make my way back up to his face, a smirk forms on his lips. It takes me a second before I realize it, glancing back down at the jersey Kaylee tossed me to wear, noticing we're both wearing the same number.

"Of course, you gave me Jaxsen's number," I mutter.

She laughs. "I can't believe you didn't even think to ask or check. His name is on the back too."

"What?" I scoff.

He bounces the ball between his legs, back and forth, before he flashes me a wink. He goes up for a jump shot, shooting the ball and finishing it with a swish of the net.

I have no words, but something about watching him play, the confidence oozing out of him, is so very attractive.

The energy in the arena is electric throughout the entire game. It took Jaxsen a while to loosen up and get into a groove, but by the start of the second quarter, he is knocking down shots left and right.

Miami is down going into halftime. I can sense Jaxsen is on edge. His face is stoic, and his jaw is set, reminding me of the no-nonsense Jaxsen I first met in New York.

A few times, I find myself gritting my teeth, anxiety zipping through me, especially with some of the players on the other team being aggressive. It's clearly getting under Jaxsen's skin too.

At one point, Sydney mentioned how Colson tries to keep him calm when it gets too physical. Kaylee ended up telling me during halftime about his history of erupting when it happens, and it's never turned out well for him.

The rest of the game seems to fly by quickly. Miami makes a comeback, knocking down shot after shot, bringing us to the last two minutes of the game.

"Everyone is on edge about this game," Kaylee mutters.

"Why?" I lean my head toward her.

"If they win this game, the Blaze take over the top seed and will move onto the next round. They'd face Brooklyn. If they make it past them, there's a chance Miami will play Jaxsen's biggest rival, Crew Savage."

"Biggest rival?"

"Let's just say they have a history of getting too physical with each other."

"Yeah, and the last time it almost cost him his career," Sydney adds.

My brows shoot up.

As she says it, one of Milwaukee's players goes up for a shot, and Jaxsen follows behind him. His hand shoots out to swat the ball away from the rim.

The crowd erupts around us, sending everyone to their feet, cheering and clapping.

Jaxsen bounces on his feet, clenching his fist, and beats it against his chest. The sounds of sirens swarm around us as the referee blows his whistle.

Jaxsen's excitement disappears, quickly jogging over to the announcer's table.

"Oh no," Kaylee mutters.

Players from Miami swarm around Jaxsen again, pulling him back. He shouts something, attempting to push his way back toward the table. He says something, pointing at one of the referees before they blow their whistle.

"Jaxsen, damn you. Sit the hell down!" Sydney shouts. "He's gonna get ejected again if he doesn't calm down."

This time, when Jaxsen turns to stalk back toward the Blaze bench, he looks up at me, and I could swear I see him relax a little. He takes a deep breath and shakes his head, attempting to let it go.

"Thank God Rush is here to talk some sense into him," Kaylee shouts.

I'm still trying to piece together what happened when the crowds' cheers quickly shift to a loud, roaring boo.

"The refs are saying he hit the other player in the arm, calling a foul. It means Jaxsen has six fouls. If he gets one more, he's out of the game."

"What the hell? Are you kidding?"

It's as if Jaxsen can hear me talking. His arms raised above his head, pacing back and forth, he turns back toward me.

I don't know why I have it in my mind he can hear me, but in the moment, I want to reassure him it's okay. I mouth the words to him, and he nods as if knowing what I said.

I flash him a smile, following it up with, "You got this."

He nods again, turning away from us, dropping his arms to his side.

The last two minutes feel like they tick by slowly. Miami is down by two points. Now isn't the time to let Jaxsen's temper get the best of him, especially when he's been playing great all night.

I still don't know a damn thing about basketball, and I'm struggling to keep up with what's happening, but I do know one thing, it's a damn good thing every time he knocks down another shot.

I'm on pins and needles, holding my breath each time one of the Blaze players shoots or goes up for a rebound. The crowd starts to chant, "Let's Go Blaze," and I join in with them. They grow louder and louder each time.

I squeeze my hands into a fist as the last ten seconds of the game fall. Milwaukee is up by one point. Jaxsen lets the ball roll slowly on the floor. Once he reaches mid-court, he picks it up and bounces it between his legs.

He shouts something to his team, sending them moving around the court.

Jaxsen makes a quick pass and I hear Sydney next to us shout for Colson to shoot it. He's standing off to the side of the court, facing us, left open with his hands in the air. He quickly goes up for the shot when another player comes out of nowhere, attempting to block him. He manages to pass the ball back to Jaxsen.

I'm scared to check the clock out of fear it's too late when Jaxsen goes up for the shot. I clutch my hands into fists so tight, I feel my nails dig into my skin. As if in slow motion, the ball soars to the hoop. It bounces on the rim once, twice, before it finally drops in as the buzzer rings out.

I shoot my hands up in the air, jumping up and down, and the arena erupts in cheers. A bullhorn sounds, and music blares through the speakers.

I can't fight off the grin stretching across my face at the sight of Jaxsen and the rest of the team jumping around like kids, celebrating their win.

When Jaxsen turns his attention back to me, he catches me with the same smile beaming on my face. He points his finger at me, nodding his head as if saying, "I see you."

"You still want to pretend like there's no history between the two of you?" Kaylee smirks.

How do I tell her it was a long story?

Actually, it wasn't. It's just one I'd have to save for another night.

CHAPTER NINE

JAXSEN

Candyce: Don't forget you have your final suit fitting today at noon so don't be late.

Oh, I hadn't forgotten, and I most certainly wouldn't be late. After I saw Emmy at the game, wearing my jersey, I haven't been able to get the thought of her out of my mind.

After the way things ended in New York, to the tension between us when I went for my first fitting, I hadn't expected to see her at our game. Wearing my jersey, no less.

She can keep playing it off like she's not interested, but her reaction every time she sees me tells a different story.

I shrug my gym bag onto my shoulder and head out of the locker room, past the practice gym. I spot my teammate, Rush, standing outside our coach's office.

Everyone on the team has heard about how Rush is seeing Coach Carr's daughter. Even if he wants to pretend like it's a rumor and they're friends, we all know it to be true.

Why is everyone choosing to deny what's right in front of them?

"See ya, Rush." I nod toward him. "Coach."

I've been doing my best to keep my head down and focus on the game, not wanting to pull myself into more drama or create a distraction for me or my team. The playoffs are underway, and the last thing I want, or need, is something jeopardizing our chances or putting me in hot water.

They both tilt their heads toward me, and Rush lifts his phone in his hand, signaling for me to hit him up later.

I step out into the warm summer air and pull my aviators out, pushing them on to shield my eyes from the piercing rays. I chose to drive myself today, giving my driver, Greg, the day off. There's nothing better after an intense practice than turning up the music and freeing my mind.

Twenty minutes later, I'm pulling the door open to Michael Jacobs. The door chimes when I enter. I don't miss how Emmy's gaze quickly darts toward the door, as if expecting me, or the way her eyes light up when she sees me.

She knew I was coming; we arranged the appointment the last time I was here. I can't help but wonder if the glint of happiness in her eye is because of me.

I spot the bouquet of flowers I sent her on the table near the front. She finishes with an older gentleman before turning her attention on me. When I step up to the counter, I flash her a wink.

"Thank you for the flowers." She grins. "The card was a nice touch too."

"I don't think I'll ever get over the sight of you wearing my jersey."

Her cheeks turn a bright shade of pink, and she shakes her head.

"I'll grab your suit for you. I'll be right back." She turns and disappears into the backroom.

I take the opportunity to check out her ass, those curves sending my heart beating into a tailspin. She's wearing a black dress, showing off her tan skin and toned arms, paired with a gold pair of heels. Her hair is pulled up into a clip, with strands falling around her face.

Her ass and those legs, though, are enough to bring a grown man to his knees.

I'm still trying to control my thoughts when she steps out of the backroom a moment later, carrying the suit with her. She hangs it on the hook at the end of the counter as she begins typing on the computer before reading me my total.

I reach into my pocket and pull out my wallet to hand her my card.

"Does this mean you're living in Miami now? What happened to you working for the airline?"

She looks up at me from under her long lashes. "I'm only here for the summer. When my internship is over, I'll be heading back to Chicago. I still work for the airline on the weekends, and during the week, I'm here."

My chest pangs learning her time here has an expiration date.

She takes in my reaction to the news. A part of me wonders if she wants it to bother me as much as it does.

"I guess that means I'm gonna have to work on convincing you to give me your number, so I can make the most of the time while you're here."

A slow smile spreads across her face, her signature blush highlighting the apples of her cheeks.

"I have a gala coming up next weekend. I know this is last minute, but if you can get the time off, I'd love to have you accompany me."

She sucks in a sharp breath, considering it.

"Next weekend?"

I nod. "Saturday night. I'll be by to pick you up around seven."

"I will have to get someone to cover my shift, but I think I can sort something out."

I reach into my pocket and pull out my phone, scrolling to her name. I still have the contact saved, for some reason. I couldn't bring myself to delete it, as ridiculous as it sounds.

"Save your number for me." I smirk. "This time, don't be sending me to any of your other ex-boyfriends or that friend of yours either."

She giggles. "What? You don't want to take Cody with you instead?"

I shake my head. "He looks like he'd chew me up and spit me out."

Emmy throws her head back, folding her hand over her mouth to contain her laughter.

"I'm gonna tell him you said that too."

"Or don't." I chuckle. "I don't need you encouraging him or giving him any ideas."

"He can be a little intense sometimes, but he's the best friend I could ever ask for."

"Only a little?"

She snickers and rolls her eyes. She reaches for my phone and types her phone number in, sliding it back across the counter. I look at the number, noticing the heart she added to her name.

I quickly fire off a text and hear her phone vibrate on the counter. The screen flashes, showing an incoming text, and she picks it up.

"See." She holds her phone up, showing me the message saying, "hi beautiful" from my number. "Don't worry, it's me."

Later that night, I'm lying in bed, watching ESPN when my phone vibrates on my nightstand. I pick it up and see her name flash on my screen.

Emmy: I was able to get my shift covered. Saturday night I'm all yours.

My dick hardens, immediately wishing she were lying here next to me. I start to picture her spread out in front of me again, her soft thighs pressed against the side of my face, and the taste of her sweet juices on my tongue.

Fuck.

I reach into my boxers and stroke my dick once before forcing myself to stop. I haven't gotten any since that night, and the urge to invite her over right now and end this dry spell is killing me.

I don't want us to start off like this, no matter how badly I want to sink inside her again.

Me: All mine? Don't give me any more ideas.

Emmy: Well, what do you have in mind?

She knows exactly what she's doing.

Me: If you were all mine, you'd be in my bed underneath me right now.

I stare at the screen and watch the message change from "Delivered" to "Read." The bubble appears, indicating she's typing before it stops. It starts back up again, only to stop a few seconds later.

I tilt my head back against the headboard, wondering what she'd say or how her body would respond to me if she were here right now. My phone vibrates in my hand again, and I open the message to reveal a picture of her. My cock stiffens at the sight.

It's modest but sexy, showing off her tan legs crossed and the curve of her thigh up toward her ass. It's hard telling from this angle if she's wearing underwear or not.

I want nothing more than to fall to my knees in front of her and find out for myself.

Me: Don't tease me, Emmy.
Emmy: Text me your address and I won't.

Oh, fuck.

I spring out of bed and rake my hand through my hair. I showered when I got home from practice an hour ago. I quickly type out my address before her message comes through saying, "see you soon."

I stare down at my dick, already threatening to break through my boxer briefs, begging for some relief. I quickly jump in the shower again, desperately needing to jerk off. If I have any chance of lasting more than five minutes, I will need to release a little pressure first.

I'm dressed in a pair of sweats when I hear her soft knock on the door twenty minutes later. I already know it's her before I even glance in the peephole. The concierge called a couple minutes ago requesting permission to let her up.

I click the lock on the door and swing it open to find her standing in front of me. She's wearing the same black dress from earlier today with those gold fuck-me heels.

There's no doubt in my mind I'm going to have her keep those on too.

I reach for her hand, slip her fingers between mine, and pull her inside. A devious smile curls at the edge of her lips.

When the door shuts, I bend down to lift her into my arms.

She wraps her legs around my waist, grinding her heat against me. My hands grip her ass, and I pull my hand back to smack it. She tilts her forehead against mine and drags her tongue over my lips before kissing me softly. Her nails rake through my hair, tugging on the strands, and I respond with a low hiss.

"I'm here now and waiting for you to tell me what you plan to do to me."

I carry her into my room and set her on the edge of my bed. Her legs hang over the side. She folds one over the other. I bite my lip, staring down at her in appreciation.

I lean forward and she falls back onto her elbows, pulling me with her, tilting her head up to kiss me. This isn't one of those sweet kisses either.

No, this kiss is fueled with enough passion to light a fire.

She nips and sucks my lower lip into her mouth. I reach my hand up and wrap it around her throat. She rolls her eyes shut and tilts her head back, releasing a low and throaty moan in appreciation.

I kiss her again before pulling back to lift her dress. She moves to stand, turning so I can unzip it before letting the material fall to the floor at her feet.

She bends down to unhook her heels.

"Keep them on."

Tilting her head up, she looks at me and smirks.

"I want your heels and nails digging into my back when I sink into your tight pussy."

She bites her lips and releases a heavy breath before standing, turning to face me.

Gripping her chin, I kiss her before pushing her back onto the bed. Reclining onto her elbows, she grins and slowly drags her hand up her thigh, over her stomach, and up to cup her breast.

"Tell me what you want," she murmurs, tracing her tongue along her lower lip. Her cheeks turn rosy, but she doesn't let it deter her.

Thoughts swirl in the back of my mind, thinking about all the ways I want to make her turn red for me. I want nothing more than to sink my face into her ass or fuck her hard while I smack her cheeks from behind. All those thoughts are pushed out of my mind when I think about her pretty lips wrapped around me.

"I want to fuck your mouth."

Her chest heaves and she nods, crawling back toward me. I bend down and kiss her once more before she turns over on her back, leaning her head over the side of the bed.

Oh, hell yes.

She continues to cup her breasts in her hands, pinching her nipples while she watches me untie my sweatpants, dropping them to the floor.

I tighten my lips around her nipple, licking and sucking the tight bud into my mouth. Fisting my dick in her soft hand, she flicks her tongue over the tip. My entire body goes rigid.

I'm thankful I rubbed one out before she got here; otherwise, this would've been over quickly.

She's at the perfect height this way. When I slowly slide into her mouth, there's no containing the string of curse words flowing out of my mouth.

I pull back, testing how much she can take.

"Fuck me," she mutters, tempting me.

I grip her chin in between my fingers and lean forward to kiss her.

"You're fuckin' perfect," I say, kissing her again.

I stand back up, lining my dick to sink between her tight lips. I pull back slowly before sliding in deeper this time. She holds onto my legs, urging me on.

"Mmm, fuck," I moan.

Reaching my hand out to wrap around her throat, I can tell she loves it, earning me another low groan, vibrating against my hand and around my dick.

"Jesus, baby, that feels so fuckin' good."

This time when I pull out, I don't hold back, fucking her mouth harder.

"Good girl," I hum as she tightens her lips, sucking me.

I died and went to heaven with this girl.

Fuck me if this isn't the best way to go.

CHAPTER TEN

EMMY

"Do you plan on seeing him again before your date?" Cody asks as he wheels the cart back toward the cabin.

My eyes are heavy, and my feet are aching. I'd give anything to crawl into bed right now.

It's Sunday afternoon, and we're on the last leg of our shift, heading back to Miami. I knew when I accepted this internship, it was going to make for an exhausting three months. Not only was I giving up my summer, but it meant long days with little to no sleep.

"I don't know. We don't have plans, so probably not."

"I still can't believe he invited you to the gala with him."

My stomach twists into a knot. The thought of surrounding myself with all these big names and celebrities sends my anxiety into a tailspin. Everything about his world was out of my element. Some days I still want to pinch myself knowing I'm working with a designer like Michael Jacobs, but this is something else entirely.

"Did he tell you what it's for?" Cody pries.

I collapse back into my seat and reach for my bottle of water, taking a large swig.

"Kaylee let it slip that he's accepting an award, but I have no idea what it's for. He didn't tell me, though, just said it's a gala."

Cody claps enthusiastically, earning some curious glances our way. He pulls the curtain closed, separating us from the rest of the passengers, and takes the seat next to me.

"Have you tried looking him up online?"

I kick my feet up on the footrest in front of me and attempt to get comfortable. There's hardly any space, though, making it impossible to relax.

I shake my head. "No. I kinda like the thought of not knowing anything about that part of his world."

"You have no idea why he was in New York that day, do you?"

My brows shoot up, immediately jumping to conclusions. Why is it that I always expect the worst from everyone, especially men?

Probably because I've been let down by them repeatedly throughout my life. My parents divorced when I was young. Although sharing custody, splitting our time every other weekend, he flaked on it more times than I could count.

After finding out about the lies Matthew kept from me, I find myself wanting to keep a wall up to protect myself from whatever this is with Jaxsen.

He's a basketball player. He's sexy and could have his pick of a whole roster of women. What could he possibly want with me?

"Your man got himself into some hot water after getting into a fight with another player."

My mouth falls open, and I shoot up straight. "I mean, I heard he has a history of getting aggressive, but I didn't realize it got that bad. Are you serious?"

He nods. "You got yourself a bad boy." He wags his brows and drags his teeth over his lower lip.

I smirk. "What did he do?"

"Trash talking each other, and it went too far." He shrugs. "Although there are rumors they have a beef off the court, with an ex of his; that could be making it worse."

"Explain."

"I guess Jaxsen was seeing some blonde Barbie. From what I could find, no one knows exactly what went down, but she popped up a few weeks after their rumored split with the same player, Crew Savage."

I remember the name. It's the same player Kaylee brought up at the game. My chest pangs at the thought of Jaxsen with someone else.

Blonde Barbie? What could I possibly have in common with someone like that?

I reach into my purse tucked underneath our seat and grab my phone, swiping my screen to disable airplane mode.

"Are you going to message him?" Cody asks.

"I'm curious who she is," I mutter, rolling my lips together.

My phone vibrates in my hand, as a series of iMessages roll through. I notice a couple of them from my mom and Kaylee, but my eyes zero in on the ones from Jaxsen.

Jaxsen: We won.

Jaxsen: One more win and we're onto Round Two. Wish you could've been here.

I didn't know a damn thing about basketball until Jaxsen filled me in on how the playoffs work. I guess they have three rounds before they can make it to the finals. They're still on their second round.

My mind drifts back to what Kaylee said at their game, about it being likely Jaxsen will face his biggest rival, Crew Savage.

They've been killing it this round, winning the first three games out of the seven-game series.

Me: That's amazing, baby. We'll have a lot to celebrate this weekend.

The message changes to read within seconds before the bubble appears, indicating he's typing. My heart leaps in my chest.

Cody pulls out his phone, and his fingers quickly zip across the screen. It's almost unreal how fast he can type on that thing.

A few seconds later, he taps the screen and turns it to face me. A picture of a blonde girl with legs for days is pulled up, her arm wrapped around Jaxsen's waist.

She's beautiful, blonde, with perfect teeth and a bright smile. She reminds me of Blake Lively, and something about that thought fills the pit of my stomach with jealousy.

Jaxsen, though, looks different. His eyes look devoid of emotion, his jaw set. He's nothing like the sweet Jaxsen I've grown to know since living in Miami.

I take in their body language and the way his hand holds her waist against him, her chest pressed against his.

"Wow," I murmur. "She's beautiful."

"Nuh uh," Cody wags his finger. "We won't be doing that, girly. Don't you be comparing yourself to her. She may be beautiful on the outside, but she's no match for you, girlfriend. You're the total package. You're just as amazing on the outside as you are on the inside."

My face softens, and I rest my head against his shoulder. "You're the best friend a girl could ever ask for."

"You bet your sweet ass I am. Write that down too. Don't you forget it."

I giggle and turn my attention back to my text messages with Jaxsen.

"What's he saying?" Cody asks, turning to eavesdrop on our conversation.

I hold my phone to my chest. "No way, get back." I snicker. "All he said was they won their game."

He rolls his eyes. "I fill you in on all the juicy gossip, and you can't even share the goods in return?"

There's nothing to hide with Jaxsen, but I also know Cody isn't one to keep quiet. If I were to let something slip about our conversations, Lord knows it would only be a matter of time before he does the same when Jaxsen's around.

I want to keep some things left between the two of us, even though Cody is my best friend and knows everything there is about me.

Or maybe I'm just trying not to get too attached to Jaxsen. I'm still trying to remember to keep this fun and enjoy our time together. No strings attached.

Before too long, I'll be packing up and moving back to Chicago, and we'll go back to what we were before our night in New York.

Jaxsen: Why wait until this weekend?

The message rolls through before Carter's voice comes over the loudspeaker, announcing we're approaching the Miami-Dade airport.

I shove my phone into my purse and quickly stand. The move causes my vision to blur, and my stomach rolls. I slap my hand over my mouth. Cody's hand darts out to help steady me.

"Are you all right?" His voice has an edge of panic in his tone.

"Yeah." I nod. "I think I'm just tired and need to eat something."

"Sit down, baby, sit down." He urges, his hands out ready to catch me at any moment. "Eat some crackers for me. I'll take this last round, okay?"

He hands me a stack of crackers and another bottle of water before he disappears behind the curtain, leaving me to a moment alone.

I've always been prone to migraines, some so bad they cause my vision to blur, and I get dizzy. I've tried numerous medications in the past, even went as far as getting

Botox injections in my scalp to get relief. They've improved over the years, but boy when they hit me, they hit hard.

I finish my pack of saltines and toss the wrapper in the wastebasket. I'm starting to feel better. I muster up enough energy to finish off the rest of my shift.

After we deplane all the passengers, we run through our post-flight checklist.

"Do you want me to give you a ride home?" Cody asks, as we take the ramp back to the airport. Carter is two steps behind me, his eyes glued to his phone.

"No." I shake my head. "I have my rental parked here, and I need it, so I have a ride for my shift at MJ's tomorrow."

His eyes are full of concern. He still has one more flight tonight, but I know if I were to tell him I needed a ride, he'd find someone to cover his shift, and he'd take me home.

Cody is aware of my history with migraines and the issues they've caused. One time we were out to dinner with co-workers for a holiday party when one came on. I wasn't drinking or anything. Everything went black, and I stumbled, sending me falling and I narrowly missed the tall bar table behind me.

I know he's only looking out for me and is worried something like that could happen.

"I'll text you when I get home. Promise," I reassure him, adjusting my purse on my shoulder.

I can't wait to get home and take this stuffy uniform off and climb into my bathtub. It's been nonstop go, go, go. I have the rest of the evening to myself and fully intend to order some food and curl up on the couch to watch *Grey's Anatomy.*

I've been catching up on the episodes after watching it a few seasons back. After I watched the airplane episode, I boycotted the show entirely before my friend, Haelynn, from back home, urged me to watch it again.

Cody walks with me out to my car. We round the corner in the airport, heading out the doors toward the parking lot when I spot a man standing near the entrance. He's leaning against the brick pillar, dressed in a pair of black shorts and a red T-shirt, a baseball cap pulled down shielding his eyes.

I suck in a sharp breath, and my step falters, sending Cody spinning around in a panic. I hold my hand out and mutter under my breath, "I'm okay."

His nostrils flare before his gaze follows mine, landing on Jaxsen.

"Well, well, well … if it isn't the bad boy himself." Cody chuckles.

Jaxsen tilts his head up and walks toward me. His brows narrow in question, but I wave it off, trying to play it off like it's Cody being Cody.

My eyes shoot over to Cody, silently telling him to shut up.

"I've been called worse, I guess," Jaxsen jokes.

"I wasn't expecting to see you here." I glance at him, while his fingers are gripping my hips, pulling me into him.

"I knew you were just coming in, and I thought you may be hungry. I was hoping I could catch you before you head home. Maybe we could grab dinner?"

"You should probably get her home, honestly," Cody interjects.

"Why?" Jaxsen questions, picking up the concern in his voice.

"It's nothing. I just wasn't feeling well on the flight back, and Cody is looking out for me. He's worried about me driving, but I've assured him it's nothing to be worried or stressed over."

"Promise me, you'll make sure she gets home and eats. She's been on the go too much and needs to slow her ass down."

"Do me a favor, will ya?" Jaxsen asks Cody.

He bends down and slips his arms beneath my legs, lifting me into his arms. He catches me off guard, my arms circling his neck to hold on. He mumbles under his breath, "I got you. What, did you think I was gonna drop you?"

I shake my head, catching the subtle smell of his cologne mixed with his clean scent.

"Grab her suitcase for me and bring it over to my car."

He carries me across the parking lot to where his black Maserati is parked. He sets me down on the ground and reaches into his pocket for his keys. He hits the unlock button, the lights flash, and he opens the door, watching as I climb inside.

When I move to pull the seatbelt over my lap, he bends down and leans inside, taking the buckle from me.

"I'm capable of buckling myself, ya know."

His lip curls in a small grin. "I know."

He takes the buckle and pushes it in until it clicks. His face is only a few mere inches away from mine, his warm breath heating my skin. I squeeze my legs together, trying to hide the fact his closeness is doing crazy things to my insides.

He leans forward, brushing his nose against mine before our lips meet. It's slow at first before his mouth opens, his tongue coaxing mine to follow. When his tongue brushes against mine, I let out a quiet moan.

He pulls back, his eyes heavy with desire.

"I missed this," he whispers. "I missed you."

He stands, shutting the door behind him. The window is cracked, and I hear him thank Cody for taking care of me. He takes the handle to my suitcase and loads it up into the trunk before climbing in next to me.

I turn to him and ask, "Where are we going?"

"You'll see," he smiles, putting the car in drive. The engine revs to life, sending a spurt of adrenaline coursing through me.

I was looking forward to a quiet night at home, but that was until Jaxsen showed up.

"You're really not gonna tell me?"

His voice drops as he says, "Don't you worry, sweetheart. I promise I'll be taking good care of you."

It's the promise behind those words that sends my stomach fluttering again.

CHAPTER ELEVEN

JAXSEN

"Mmm ..." she hums. "He cooks."

Her quiet footsteps pad across the kitchen floor. When I turn my head to glance over my shoulder, I find her dressed in my T-shirt and gym shorts I left out on the bed for her. Her wet hair is tussled, tossed waywardly like she ran her fingers through the long strands.

She folds her arms around her waist, inhaling a deep breath as she eyes the food cooking on the stove.

Originally, I tried to sell her on soup after hearing Cody insist that she wasn't feeling well. She reassured me she was feeling better and has been craving pasta.

When we got back to my place, I set her up with a warm bath surrounded by candles while I got to work on dinner. We have both been running nonstop, and I knew she could use some time to relax. I've become so accustomed to eating dinner alone, I welcomed the chance to cook for her.

"I'm a man of many talents." I grin, brushing the back of my hand over her cheek.

She sighs and takes a step closer to me. She unties her arms around her and circles them around my waist.

"I can see that already." She smiles warmly up at me.

I've never thought I'd be so attracted to a woman in all the ways I'm attracted to her. Every curve of her body, the sight of her wearing no makeup, even her wearing my clothes has me nearly coming undone.

"The shrimp alfredo is almost done. Will you grab us a couple plates and silverware?" I ask, motioning toward the cabinet before stepping away to grab the salad left in the fridge.

She sets everything out on the counter and takes a seat across the island on one of the barstools. She stretches her legs out on the chair next to her, crossing her feet at her ankles.

My eyes linger on her toned legs and bronzed skin. My mouth goes dry, dragging my tongue over my lips to wet them.

"I don't know whether to be turned on from the sight of you cooking for me or the look in your eyes. What are you thinking about?"

I curl the edge of my mouth in a smile.

"I should probably wait until after we eat to answer."

Her brows shoot up, she tilts her head in a narrowing gaze. "Why is that?"

"I just spent the last twenty minutes cooking this de-licious dinner for you. If we venture down that road, I'm afraid it'll be left cold while I spread you out on the island and eat you instead."

She sucks in a sharp breath, and I grin.

I lift the pan, scooping a portion of alfredo onto her plate, and top it with shrimp before doing the same to my own. I add some lettuce, setting the dressing on the table next to us, and carry her plate over to her.

Her eyes light up and she murmurs a quiet thank you, tilting her head up for a kiss. I lean forward and press my lips to hers, my hand skating over her stomach, brushing underneath her breasts.

She trembles from my touch, and I pull back to stop myself from pushing it any further. She blinks through the haze of desire in her eyes, and I flash her a wink.

"You have a way of making me forget where I'm at or what I'm doing." She sighs.

I pick up my plate and circle the island, taking the seat next to her. She moves to pull her legs back, when I stop her, lifting them before resting them back in my lap.

"Is that a good thing?"

She chuckles and shrugs, twirling noodles around her fork before taking a large bite. Her eyes flutter closed, and she moans through a heavy sigh.

The sight of her, her cheeks rosy and the light smattering of freckles on her face makes my dick hard. She wants to talk about me being a distraction. Has she thought about how she looks right now or the fact her foot is dangerously close to where my dick is now pressed against the waistband of my shorts?

"On second thought, I think I've figured out the answer. If you keep making noises like that or roll your eyes closed again, I'm going to say forget dinner and find better ways of making you do the same thing."

She presses her lips together to cover her smile and moves her foot, brushing against my dick. I hiss, dropping my fork to my plate.

"You make it very hard to remember how to behave, Emmy."

"What if I don't want you to be good?"

My nostrils flare, my eyes flicking to the sauce leftover on her lips. She drags her tongue along them, causing my brain to falter trying to formulate a response.

"Eat," I command, and she bites her lip, this time not hiding the fact her mouth is stretched wide in a smile.

I shake my head, turning back toward my food.

We both sit in silence, eating before she attempts to change the subject. I mentally force myself not to think about her foot in my lap or the thought of lifting her in my arms, carrying her back to my room.

We chat about her last shift at work and how she believes today was spurred on because she hasn't slept well recently. She asks me about when my next game is and promises to watch even if she can't be there to cheer me on.

When we finish eating, she takes my plate from me and carries it with hers to the sink, washing them off before adding them to the dishwasher.

Coming up behind her, I wrap my arms around her waist and pull her into me. She sighs and tilts her head back, closing her eyes when I trail my fingers over her stomach and up to cup her breast.

She's not wearing a bra, so when I brush my thumb over her nipple, the sensation causes her body to shudder. She reaches her hand up to hold onto my wrist. I continue my path, over her chest to her shoulders, massaging them as her body relaxes. She tilts her head to the side, and I lean in feathering kisses along her collarbone and up the column of her neck.

"Mmm," she moans. "That feels wonderful."

"I told you, Em, I'm a man of many talents. I've been told I'm good with my hands."

She chuckles, turning in my arms to wrap hers around my neck. She pulls me down and kisses me, and I lift her onto the edge of the counter.

Her hands fold against the side of my face as she circles her legs around my waist to hold me close to her. When I slowly grind my hips against her, she moves her hand down to grip my chin.

"Jaxsen ..." she trails off. "I don't want you to be good anymore."

I reach up, plucking her nipple through the cotton of her shirt. Her body jolts, her mouth falling open as her stare bores into me.

She releases a shuttered breath.

"I don't think you know what you're getting yourself into, Emmy."

She leans forward, her gaze never breaking contact with mine. Her finger skates over my stomach and down to my dick, curving her hand to stroke me through my shorts.

"Oh, I do," she whispers. "I'm just waiting for you to break and give me what I want."

Slipping my hands under her thighs, I lift her into my arms and carry her down the hall toward my room.

She trails her tongue over my collarbone before nipping and sucking her way up my neck. The suction intensifies, nearly enough to break the skin. I drop her on the edge of the bed, and she falls back giggling.

I reach for the hem of her shorts, dragging them with her panties down her legs in one swift move. The move causes her laughter to stop as she stares up at me in surprise.

"Is this what you want?" I ask.

She stays quiet, following me as I drop to the floor between her legs and turn my attention to her pussy. I can see how wet she is even in the dimly lit room. Only the lamp on the bedside table is left on from when she was in here after her bath.

She pushes herself up onto her forearms, staring down her body at me, but doesn't utter a word.

"Emerson," I command, reaching my hand out to pinch her clit.

Her mouth drops open at the same time her thighs fall to the side. The look on her face is a mix of not knowing whether she likes the pain or if she wants to beg me to do it again.

"What was the question?" She shakes her head as if shaking herself from her thoughts. Her eyes blink slowly.

"Sit up."

She obeys. She reaches for the hem of her shirt and pulls it over her head, tossing it at me, landing on my face.

I reach up and pull the material away, and the look on my face sends her in a fit of laughter.

"You're gonna get it." I smirk.

She crawls up the bed and I stalk after her, shedding my shirt in the process. Her laughter stops when I push her legs back, bending her body in half, leaving her spread open beneath me.

"Jaxsen," she murmurs.

I don't take my eyes off her when I lean down, dragging my tongue from her pussy toward her clit. She moves her hands to grip my hair, holding me against her as she struggles to breathe.

Each slow movement from her pussy toward her clit and back down has her chest heaving, the muscles in her thighs flexing while she attempts to hold on.

When I pull back, adding a finger to the mix, and flick my tongue over her clit, she pushes my head down, attempting to grind against my face. The sounds of her muffled moans intermixed with her body trembling have me nearly coming.

I want to feel her wet pussy around me when she cums.

I release my grip on her legs and brush my thumb over her clit while I finger her, licking and sucking my way up toward her nipples.

"My turn." She grins, reaching her hand out to brush over the front of my shorts.

She knows exactly what she's doing. She's letting me call the shots, but each and every time she touches me, I find myself giving in to her a little more.

Who the hell does she think she is?

Standing next to the bed, I drop my shorts to the floor and climb over her body. She's leaning against a stack of pillows on the bed, dragging her bottom lip between her teeth.

I hold onto the headboard, positioning my dick at her mouth.

"Open your fuckin' mouth, Emerson."

She stares up at me underneath her long lashes and follows my direction.

I start out slow at first, smacking the tip of my dick on her tongue before slowly sliding inside. When I hit the back of her throat, she moans around me. I let off a string of curse words attempting to keep some semblance of control.

One stroke and she nearly has me coming undone.

She drags her nails up my thighs, holding onto me. I reach for her hands, crossing her wrists to hold her in place as I pull back and thrust into her mouth.

She wiggles beneath me, rubbing her legs together.

"Keep your legs open." I smirk, reaching behind me to rub her clit.

"Jaxsen, you're killing me."

"Oh, I'm killing you now? What do you think you're doing to me?"

I pinch her clit again, and she bucks her hips. I free her hands and she grins. She wastes no time reaching out to wrap her soft hand around my dick, jerking me off in one swift move.

"Fuuuccckkk," I moan.

I collapse on the bed next to her.

"Get on this dick, baby. Right now."

Her eyes light up with desire, moving over to straddle me.

This time when she slides down on me, her wet pussy gripping me like it's coming for my life, it's me who rolls my eyes shut.

"Good girl." I smirk. "Now fuck me like the good girl you are."

CHAPTER TWELVE

EMMY

Two knocks hit the door, and I suck in a sharp breath. I wring my hands out to release the wave of anxiety shuddering through me. My heels click on the hardwood floor as I cross through my apartment and flip the lock. Jaxsen is standing on the other side, dressed in his suit.

His mouth curves up on the sides in a devious grin, his eyes slowly traveling down my body. My hand nervously runs over the front of my red dress.

When Kaylee heard I was accompanying Jaxsen as his date, she insisted on helping me pick out the perfect dress. Until I told her about a dress I designed six months ago, intending to wear it for my anniversary with Matthew, only the time never came. It's sat untouched in my closet all this time, never seeing the light of day. It's the perfect dress for this occasion.

Looking at Jaxsen now, the way his eyes drink in every inch of my body, something tells me there's a reason things happened the way they did. This dress deserves to be appreciated in only the way Jaxsen does. Although the look on his face right now says he's resisting the urge to say let's forget about our plans for the evening.

"My God ..." His voice trails off.

I giggle, brushing my hand over the material again. I'm a bit ashamed to admit I've added a few pounds, making it even tighter than I remember it being before, but it still looks beautiful. If it means stuffing myself into a pair of Spanx to witness the look on his face, it was well worth it.

"You like?" I smile, doing a quick spin. His eyes linger on the curve of my ass before moving down my legs. He reaches his hand out and pulls me into his arms.

"Oh baby, I more than like. You have me dyin' to rip this dress off you and drag you to your room right now."

I tilt my head back and smile, wagging my finger at him. His brows furrow.

"I'll have you know, I made this, and it's one of my favorite pieces. You will not be harming it in any way, or you'll be sorry."

His brows shoot up. "Oh, yeah? How exactly do you intend on punishing me?"

He chuckles. He has a light smattering of hair lining his jaw. My body hums at the thought of it brushing over the tender skin between my thighs.

He must sense my thoughts drifting off to more in-appropriate topics, when he reaches his hand down to grip my ass, pulling me against him, feeling his hardness through the front of his pants.

"Keep it up, and we really won't be leaving."

My chest heaves, making it difficult to catch my breath. "I will be off-limits to you. No touching, kissing, nothing."

He smiles, but this one is serious and not at all in a funny way. His voice drops low, and he says, "Baby, I think that will torture you just as much as it would me. Try again."

He's right. The rush of desire coursing through me, the way his gaze burns into my skin, and the reaction to his touch says I'm in just as much trouble as he is if I were to deny him.

I don't stand a chance, and I never did.

He laces his fingers with mine and leads me out to the waiting SUV. He nods his head to the man standing near the backdoor, holding it open for us.

"Thank you, Greg." He nods, and steps back, helping me into the backseat before walking around to the other side to join me.

Greg, his driver, climbs back into the driver's seat, our eyes meeting in the rearview mirror. He's older, old enough to be my grandfather, with a warm smile.

"Sir, we should be there in about fifteen minutes," Greg says, flicking the turn signal on before pulling out onto the street from my high-rise apartment in downtown Miami.

He thanks him again, sliding over across the seat until our thighs touch. He rests his hand on my thigh, tangling our fingers together. He lifts our hands to his mouth, tracing his lips over my skin, causing my heart to hammer in my chest.

My eyes flash to the front, meeting Greg's once more. I swear I notice a small grin playing at his mouth before he focuses his attention back on the road.

Does Jaxsen have dates often? He must get a lot of action in these backseats.

He moves our conjoined hands onto his lap, and I turn my head to stare out the window, watching the sights and sounds of the city pass us by. Jaxsen must pick up on my change in mood, pulling me by my arm to look at him.

"Hey, you feelin' okay?" he asks.

I nod. "Just nervous is all. You never did tell me what this event was for. Kaylee mentioned you were nominated for an award, but what is it for exactly?"

He looks down as if not sure how to articulate what he wants to say. Or maybe he's nervous too. I can't be quite sure.

"I'm being recognized tonight by the NBA."

"You are?" I exclaim. "You already got the award?"

He chuckles. "Yeah. Every month the league awards one player for their philanthropic and charity work, then at the end of the season, they recognize someone for the entire season."

"You got the award for the entire season?" My eyes widen. This moment feels like I'm peeling back another layer of Jaxsen Wild to a side I didn't expect to find. A deeper and softer side of him.

He nods.

"Jaxsen, that's incredible." I squeeze his fingers, wrapping my arm around him in a hug. "I'm so proud of you."

Greg pipes up from the front, sounding like a proud father when he says, "Jaxsen doesn't like to talk about himself, so I'll do him the honors. Don't believe the things you hear about him in the media. They like to make him out to be an untamed wild child. He's a good man with a giving heart. One of the best men I know."

My chest seizes and I glance over at Jaxsen, attempting to blink away the tears pricking my eyes. He shakes his head, staring out the window, as if finding it hard to believe.

I recall all the things I read the media outlets said about him. They do like to make him out to be a bad boy with a wild temper. This soft and vulnerable side I'm seeing of him is the exact opposite of what they claim him to be.

"You don't have to lie to her, Greg." Jaxsen laughs, trying to lighten the mood. "Although I certainly appreciate you putting in a good word for me."

"I only speak the truth, sir. I've spent every day with you for the last four years. Make no mistake about it, you're a good man. I'm proud of you."

"Thanks," he says shyly.

I don't know for certain, but I get a feeling Greg's praise means a lot to him.

We pull up in front of the building a few minutes later. Greg opens the door for Jaxsen first before they both join me on my side, helping me climb down. The temperatures have dropped since the sun has begun to set, disappearing behind the clouds.

The sky is a mixture of yellows, pinks, and purples. It's a stunning sight. A red carpet leads into the front entrance with photographers lining the sidewalk, snapping photos of the two of us as we walk inside. Jaxsen keeps his head down, wrapping his hand in mine, leading me toward the door, clearly having no interest in stopping for photos.

The building overlooks the water, with large windows allowing for the perfect view of the sunset. The water laps at the shore in the distance. Tables are spread throughout the room with large chandeliers and gorgeous ceilings, painted as if they were using watercolors.

Jaxsen tilts his head in greeting to a few people we meet as we make our way through the ballroom. All the men are dressed in suits and tuxedos, the women with them in stunning evening gowns and glittered with diamonds.

My nerves are hyped up, feeling out of place amongst the crowd.

There are two rows of high-top tables around the outside of the room. People stand, chatting and sipping champagne while they converse with each other. I recognize a man, taller and built like Jaxsen, with short dark hair standing next to a redheaded woman. When she turns toward us, I recognize it is Sydney, Kaylee's friend, which means the handsome man with the warm smile next to her must be Colson.

Jaxsen claps his hand, patting him on the back in a hug. "Rush, Syd, how's it going?"

"Not bad, man. Congratulations. It's well deserved."

He's older than Jaxsen by a few years.

"Means a lot coming from you," Jaxsen says, nodding.

Jaxsen motions to me. "Emmy, this is my teammate Colson Rush, and you know his girlfriend, Sydney Carr." Jaxsen playfully jabs Colson in the chest, following it up with, "I can call her your girlfriend now, right? The word is officially out?"

Colson chuckles. "Yeah, I finally convinced her to stop running away from me."

"I think I've managed to do the same with Emmy," Jaxsen says, flashing me a wink.

Sydney rolls her eyes, shaking her head. She reaches her hands out to me, pulling me into a hug.

"Nice to see you again, Emmy."

"You as well."

"You can ignore Jaxsen and his antics. Colson and I met right before I started working with my dad for the Miami Blaze. I had no idea my new neighbor happened to be one of the star players for the team, which you could understand made things a little complicated."

"Only complicated because you made them that way, sweetheart." Colson lifts her hand to his mouth and kisses the back, a devilish smirk on his face.

She jerks her hand away and narrows her eyes at him. "We both agreed we needed to focus on our careers. Remember?"

I cover my mouth, giggling at the two of them. Even though they're bickering, you can tell there's a lot of love between them.

Jaxsen's arm wraps around my waist, pulling me into his side.

"Would you like something to drink?" he asks.

"Yes, please. Whatever you're having," I say. "I'm going to step away to use the restroom. I'll be right back."

I search around the room, spotting the sign along the back wall. My feet move quickly. I've only been here for maybe twenty minutes. I used the restroom right before we left, and I already feel like my bladder is about to explode.

Ever since the flight home from my last shift, I've been trying to make changes to eat better and drink more water. I've been feeling lousy, and I'm positive that's playing a role in it. Although, all this water has me visiting the bathroom practically every hour, like clockwork.

I open the door and rush into the bathroom stall. I quickly take care of business and grab my clutch from where I hung it on the back of the door, letting it dangle from my wrist while I wash my hands.

"I never pegged Jaxsen to be into brunettes," a sweet voice mutters from behind me.

My gaze darts up to the mirror, and my eyes fall on a face I recognize, although I do my best to seem indifferent.

Blonde Barbie.

Although, if I'm honest, the photos online don't do her justice. She's even more stunning in person, which is sad, considering she's only spoken one sentence to me, and I can already tell it's the only thing going for her.

"I beg your pardon?" I quip.

"Jaxsen Wild, your date," she says. "I never thought I'd see the day when he'd have a brunette on his arm, a plus size one at that."

My mouth drops open before I quickly snap it shut. Adrenaline shoots through me like a shot of tequila, causing my body to hum and burn with intensity.

My heels click on the floor of the small bathroom. We're not alone, but a few people walking in and out of the stalls duck their heads and pretend as if they don't have eyes and ears, witnessing the sheer audacity of this woman.

"Excuse me?" I retort, grabbing two towels from the dispenser, drying off my hands.

I've never considered myself skinny, nor has anyone ever considered me to be, especially by societies standards. I never cared to be either. I've always had a curve to my waist and more than a handful in my ass, and I'm a-okay with it.

After the breakup with Matthew, I was down on myself and my body. I felt insecure, telling myself maybe if I was skinnier, prettier, or looked a certain way, maybe he wouldn't have cheated.

Maybe he would've stayed with me.

It took me a while to learn no man deserving of my love would have me questioning if I was worthy of his love in return.

"Didn't you hear me the first two times?"

"Oh, I heard you all right. I was just giving you a chance to take it back. Certainly, you're not going to stand here and have the nerve to speak about me and my body as if your opinion is worth a damn."

She curls her lip in a snarl and narrows her eyes at me.

"Don't you get it? He isn't interested in you. You're just one in a long line of women. There have been a dozen before you, and there will be plenty more after."

I chuckle. "Honey, there's only one person here who doesn't seem to get it. There's not enough makeup in the world that can cover up the ugly you carry with you on the inside."

The door swings open and I notice Sydney's red hair out of the corner of my eye, but I don't dare break eye contact with this fake bitch.

"Spewing your vile hatred certainly isn't going to make him want you either."

Sydney bursts out laughing, and I glance over to see her smiling, immediately knowing what she walked in on.

"You heard her," Sydney retorts. "Run along now."

I grin as Barbie crosses the room between us before quickly reaching for the door and disappearing outside.

"I knew I liked you." Sydney grins.

I wink. "Right back atcha."

She nods toward the door. "Jaxsen sent me in here to make sure you were okay. You weren't in need of saving, but I'm damn glad I witnessed that with my own two eyes."

She links our arms together and leads me out the door.

She reminds me of Kaylee, and with that thought alone, I know we'll get along great.

CHAPTER THIRTEEN

JAXSEN

"Can I get you a drink, sir?"

I stepped away from Colson, who was heavy in conversation with Coach Carr and another player for San Antonio, Easin Pryor, and dashed over to the bar.

I nod. "I'll take two waters, please."

The waitress smiles warmly as a hand runs up my back. I turn, expecting to find Emmy when my eyes are met with a familiar pair of ice-cold blues I hoped to never see again.

"I knew I'd see you over here." Kelly's voice drips of bitterness.

I don't miss the suggestion either. The rumor mill was swirling after the incident with Savage. Many speculated I was drinking, and it was the reason behind the change in my demeanor, both on and off the court.

It was all bullshit. There's no way I'd ever step foot on the court, or even in the arena, after having a drink. The mention of having an alcohol problem, in general, made me want to grit my teeth in anger.

"If that's the case, why are you over here? Where's your date?"

Her eyes narrow coldly. Even I can hear the anger in my voice.

I do a sweep of the room, searching for Emmy, not wanting her to catch me in this conversation. I don't have anything to hide, but I know how it looks, and Kelly is the type of person I want to keep far away from the goodness of Emmy.

We've been linked together in the past, though, so I know how it'd look if she happened to see us. I'd never go near her again, but Emmy doesn't know that, and I don't want Kelly to ruin our night together.

"Jaxsen, you know you're the only man I want to be with. Don't lie or pretend like you don't miss me too," she coos, running her hand over my front, pressing her chest against my arm.

"I thought I made it clear when I ended things exactly how I felt about us."

She rolls her eyes and sighs dramatically. "You're still mad? Jaxsy, baby. He means nothing to me."

My eyes stare past Kelly, over to Colson and Easin talking. Crew shakes Coach's hand, and I'm waiting for the moment when he looks our way.

He slips his hand in his pocket, and his eyes are surveying the room when they finally meet mine. He clenches his jaw, shaking his head when he notices who's standing in front of me.

"You might want to go tell him then. Judging by the look on his face when he just caught you talking to me, he doesn't look too happy." I chuckle.

There's nothing I'd love more than to piss Crew off, but not this way. Not with her.

Kelly sighs. "Let me come over to your place tonight and we can talk about this. It's been so long," she murmurs, running her hand over my forearm, before sliding over the front of my pants.

She releases a low moan and flutters her eyelashes at me.

"C'mon, baby, you know you miss the way I could take care of you."

I grit my teeth and grip her wrist, forcing it away from me. "Do not touch me."

The waitress sets the two glasses on the counter. I reach for my wallet, pulling out cash, and toss a tip into the jar.

"This is about *her*, isn't it?" Her voice drops to a glacier level, noting the glasses in my hand.

I knew better than to think she wanted me. This is about making sure no one else can have me.

All she wants is Jaxsen Wild, the name. The man on the court and all that comes along with it. I suspected early on she was using me for my money. She's convincing, knows how to turn it on and off, and wears the perfect mask at all the right times.

She wears it well too.

I didn't want to be with Kelly, not in the way I am with Emmy now. We both knew what this was in the beginning, and we got it in the end.

"No," I say, curtly. "In fact, it has nothing to do with her."

"So, it's because of Crew then?" She folds her arms over her chest defiantly. She looks like a child, ready to put up an argument to get what she wants.

I chuckle, moving to step around her.

"I don't want anything to do with you, Kelly. Now that I've got the chance to see the real you, I don't know why I ever did."

Her mouth falls open, a flash of hurt crossing her face.

My stomach twists in regret. I don't want to hurt her; I never did. She knew what this was, and now that I've spoken the truth, it's only a matter of time before she finds a way to make me pay for it.

"You're a jackass, Jaxsen." She grits her teeth, muttering under her breath.

A few questionable glances are shot in our direction. I lift my glass and roll my eyes, knowing exactly what everyone must think seeing the two of us together.

Anyone who listens to the gossip articles could speculate what this conversation is about.

"You can't tell me you're only finding this out now," I retort. "You'd do well to remember it too. Now, leave me the fuck alone."

My words are low and pack a punch.

She clenches her jaw as I shoulder past her, escaping into the crowd to the front of the room toward our table.

I spot Emmy and Sydney making their way through the crowd, Colson trailing behind them after he claps Easin on the shoulder. Emmy's wearing a forced smile on her face, her gaze holding mine as she saunters toward me.

Something about this reminds me of a comment Kelly made.

It's about her, isn't it?

She knows I'm here with Emmy.

I'm guessing she saw us walk in together or when we were chatting with Sydney and Colson. We've only been together a few times since New York, and when we have been together, we've kept a low profile.

"You'll never guess who we ran into in the bathroom." Sydney's lip curls in disgust.

She's never been a fan of Kelly. I didn't know why in the beginning, but I suspect it's because she could see through her and her façade.

"Who?" I ask, already knowing the answer.

I adjust my suit jacket, unbuttoning it in the front, and reach my hand out to Emmy. She slips her fingers between mine, her face softening when she looks up at me.

"Kelly."

I flick my gaze over to Sydney, before turning back to Emmy, slipping my arm around her waist. She circles her arm beneath my jacket, her body molding against my front.

"What happened?"

"Oh, you know." Sydney waves her hand. "Kelly being Kelly."

I tilt my head down, pressing my mouth against Emmy's ear. "Did she say something to you?"

"Nothing worth repeating." She sighs.

"I'm sorry you had to deal with my past. I can assure you, though, that's all she is to me. My past. You're the one I want to be with."

She tilts her head back, gazing up at me.

I've never been one to pack on the PDA, but this with Emmy is different. I don't care who is around or who may see us; I want her to know she's important to me.

I want to put all her fears and worries to rest.

Her eyes trail over my face, down to my lips. She nods, raking her teeth over her lower lip.

"If you keep looking at me like that, I'm going to kiss you right here."

"Right here?" She pushes. "Right here in front of every-one?"

I nod slowly, my eyes meeting hers before falling back on her lips.

I want to taste her so fuckin' bad. I can't wait until we get out of here so I can remind her just how much I want her.

Anytime we're around each other, it's like I can't keep my hands off her.

"Do it," she challenges me.

I faintly hear the sound of Sydney snickering behind her, but I drown it all out. I lean in and press my lips against Emmy's.

She sucks in a breath, gripping the front of my shirt in her fist as I lift my hand to cup her face. I open my mouth, brushing my tongue against hers.

"I feel like I'm interrupting something," Colson mum-bles to Sydney. "Maybe we should go somewhere. I wouldn't mind ripping that dress off you."

Emmy's body starts to shake in laughter. She pulls back and rubs her lips together, lifting her hand to her mouth, attempting to compose herself.

"You look perfect," I whisper in her ear.

"These men sure know how to sweet talk our pants right off. Don't they?" Sydney giggles, pulling out her chair. Colson steps in behind her, folding his hand over hers to do it.

"Just wait until tonight, Ms. Carr."

"Carr?" Emmy notes as I pull out her chair. "Isn't that the name of your coach you were talking to too?"

Sydney nods and Colson grins.

I take the seat next to Emmy, resting my arm along the back of her chair.

"He's my father. My parents adopted me when I was fifteen. I'm sure you noticed we look nothing alike." She chuckles.

"Your boyfriend is a player on the team your dad coaches, *and* he's your neighbor?" Emmy smiles.

She nods. "She's my favorite personal foul," Colson quips, lifting her hand to his mouth.

"You keep it up, and we'll be leaving here early."

Colson grins. Emmy glances over at me, reaching for her glass in cheers.

"Good evening," a voice booms through the speakers. "Please be seated."

The crowd begins to disperse, making their way toward their seats.

Coach Carr and his wife, Sydney's mother, join us along with Easin and a couple other players in the league who've earned the Community Cares award.

Throughout dinner, Emmy has a bright and infectious smile on her face. She makes it easy for everyone around to feel comfortable. At one point, Emmy talked about how we first met and shared how she had no idea I played basketball. I caught Coach looking in my direction with a smirk on his face.

It didn't take long before his daughter piped in too.

"You mean to tell me you got a job working for the Miami Blaze, and you still had no idea who he was?"

Colson takes a bite of his food, nearly choking, lifting a napkin to his mouth.

"I mean, of course, I'd heard of him," Sydney protests, her eyes shooting lasers at Colson. "He's one of the best three-point shooters in the NBA. I just didn't put a face to the name is all."

We all thought that was funny.

I loved how Emmy was here to support me, but she didn't care about the red carpets or the big events. I wasn't one who liked the spotlight and attention, so when it came to awards, I was ready to get this part over with.

What I cared about was knowing it brought attention to the causes close to my heart. I was given this platform, and even though the media didn't show this side, I was determined to use it for good.

"Tonight, we're here to honor one of the greatest players to grace the game, Jaxsen Wild. His size, skill, and intelligence make him an unstoppable force on the basketball court. His legacy spans just as far off the court, using his passion and influence to give back to those in need. He founded the Be Wild foundation, focusing on causes improving homelessness and education, and providing scholarships to underprivileged and minority college students. To date, he's helped more than one hundred students earn a college education through his efforts to give back."

Emmy reaches her hand beneath the table, running her palm over my thigh. I glance over at her, uncomfortable with the praise, noting the tears filling the brim of her eyes.

She lifts a napkin to her face, dabbing the corner, forcing a smile, attempting to hold her emotions together.

"We're honored to present Jaxsen Wild with the Community Cares Assist Award for his outstanding efforts in his community and ongoing charitable and philanthropic work."

The entire time I stand on stage, accepting the award, my eyes are on Emmy.

She did her best to fight off the tears, but when they handed me a check for $25,000 to the Be Wild Foundation, all hope was gone, and the tears began to flow freely down her face.

After the ceremony wraps up, I want nothing more than for us to get out of here and finally get her alone and all to myself.

I fire off a text to Greg. He responds back, letting me know he is pulling up outside.

"Sir." He nods, opening the back door for us.

"Hi Greg," Emmy croons.

"Hello, Ms. Kincaid."

"How does he know my name?" She mumbles under her breath to me as I hold my hand out, helping her in.

I chuckle, reaching over to buckle her seatbelt.

She grins, watching me buckle in.

"You're never gonna let me do it myself, are you?"

I turn my head to face her, leaving no more than an inch between us, and stare down at her lips.

"I could, but then I'd miss my chance to do this." I smirk and lean in to kiss her softly.

She flinches at the sound of photos snapping behind us before relaxing against me.

"You could've waited until we were alone, you know."

"Or you could stop being so damn irresistible, making me forget where the hell I am."

CHAPTER FOURTEEN

JAXSEN

I don't know how we managed to get lucky, but despite photos being taken of us outside of the charity event, none of them seem to surface in the days to follow.

Something shifted between us since the gala, a closeness I hadn't felt before. Although it was our first official date, the connection we share continues to grow.

We're into the second round of the playoffs. Between traveling for games and Emmy's busy schedule at the internship and the airlines, it's made it challenging for us to spend time together.

We haven't let it get in our way though. Every night we're both in Miami, we've spent it together, making dinner or watching movies. I've taken her down by the beach a few times, going on walks and watching the sunset.

This may have started off as a fling, but I don't want her to get the wrong idea and think all I want is sex, even though I can't keep my hands off her when we're together.

I'm addicted to the feel of her soft skin and curves pressed against my body, her quiet moans, and *fuck me* the way she looks when she bites her lip to muffle the sound.

When she stares up at me beneath her long lashes and smiles, I'm fuckin' done for.

We are just finishing our last game against Brooklyn. We ended up taking it to six games in the series but managed to pull out the win. Chicago beat out Indiana last night, which puts the two of us head-to-head.

The media is running wild, speculating over what will happen between the two rival teams facing each other in the playoffs.

It's no secret there's a lot of tension between our teams. I've been itching to play against Savage since my suspension toward the end of the regular season.

I need to have my head on right, focus on the game, and not let my temper get the best of me. He knows how to get under my skin, pushing every single one of my buttons.

"You ready for 'em?" Kinnick bolsters, smacking me on the chest. He grabs me by the shoulders, shaking me with a beaming smile on his face.

We were both drafted into the league together and joined the Blaze at the same time. He's one of my longest teammates and closest friends, next to Rush. Rush is older, wiser, and more of a brother to me than anything.

He's my voice of reason, talking me down whenever shit turns heated.

Kinnick, on the other hand, is just as rowdy and feisty as me. He's a smack talker and instigator who loves to get under his opponent's skin like the best of them.

"One more round, baby. One more round and we're going to the motherfuckin' finals."

"Oh, I'm ready. I've been ready." I nod, beating on my chest.

Someone flips the music on in the locker room, blaring "All I Do is Win" by DJ Khaled. I rip my jersey off and toss it into my locker.

Even in the excitement of the moment, I can't wait to get back to my hotel and tell Emmy the news. I reach into the front of my gym bag and pull out my phone, swiping through the slew of notifications from family and friends, before landing on the thread with Emmy.

Emmy: You did it, baby! You fuckin' did it!

I grin, pulling up the message, spotting a picture she sent me standing in front of her mirror wearing my jersey. It's long enough on her, it falls to mid-thigh, giving me too many ideas of all the ways I'd love to bend her over and lick her pussy while she's wearing it.

Shit.

Me: You look so damn good wearing my jersey, baby. You bring me good luck every time you do.

Emmy: I have a surprise for you when you call me tonight.

Me: Tell me.

Emmy: You'll have to wait and see.

Me: I'm too impatient to wait. Show me now.

Another picture comes through, and for a second, I'm not quite sure what I'm looking at. My finger hovers over the screen, noting the icon in the corner indicating it's a live picture. I press and hold on the screen, noticing it vibrates on her nightstand.

Did she just send me a picture of her vibrator?

"Is that what I think it is?" Miles chirps from behind me.

I press my phone against my chest, shielding it from his nosy eyes and shoot him a cursory glance over my shoulder. He holds his hand up in surrender when he notices the flare of my nostrils and the clench in my jaw.

"Whoa, I'm sorry, man. I swear, I wasn't trying to look."

I don't even want to think about him seeing her in ways meant for my eyes only.

I'd see fuckin' red.

He backs away, moving to stand in front of his locker. It's close quarters in here, reminding me to be careful about opening her pictures when curious eyes are around.

Me: Jesus! Give me thirty minutes to get back to the hotel and I'll FaceTime you.

Emmy: I'll be waiting.

As much as I'd love to stay and celebrate with the team, I'm beat. I want nothing more than to get back to my room and see Emmy.

I quickly jump in the shower to clean up and put on the suit I wore to the game. Reporters are lined up outside the locker room leading to the bus we rode on the way here, waiting to get a word.

Except I have a one-track mind.

Everything will have to wait until tomorrow. The stress of the playoffs has been mounting and all I want right now is to be with Emmy and take my mind off everything but her.

We pull up to the hotel thirty minutes later. I keep checking the clock on my phone, not wanting to keep her waiting. I have my keycard in the lock when my finger hits the call button, and Emmy's beautiful smile appears on my screen.

She's wearing a red silk tank top with lace lining the edge. Her hair is pulled up on top of her head with strands falling around her face. Her lips and cheeks are rosy, bright with a hue of desire.

"You didn't get started without me, did you?" I raise my brow, pulling my suitcase behind me, leaving it by the door.

"Maybe a little." She bites her lip and reclines back against her headboard.

She traces her finger over her lower lip, teasing me. I blink slowly, following her finger as she continues down her chin, over her chest, and between her breasts, pulling the material down to reveal her cleavage.

I suck in a sharp breath, my face heating with desire. I shrug off my suit jacket, propping my phone in front of the TV, then quickly unbutton my dress shirt.

When I open the material, giving her a hint of my tattooed chest, it's her who sighs this time.

"I wish you were here, Jaxsen."

"I do too, baby," I murmur. "I can't wait to have my hands all over your beautiful body again."

She drags her lip between her teeth as she leans up, pulling her tank top over her head. The sight of her bare breasts and her light pink nipples have my hard-on growing, fighting the urge to bust through my pants.

She licks her finger, sucking it into her mouth, before she slowly circles the tip around her nipple, causing it to tighten.

She moves to prop her phone up before she reclines back, grinning, giving me the perfect angle of her body.

I catch sight of her tan skin beneath her red pajama shorts. I want more than anything to kiss my way up her inner thigh, pull her shorts down, and bury my face between her legs until I taste her juices on my lips.

She picks up her toy I recognize from her message earlier, flips it on, and it hums to life. She runs the tip over her breast, releasing a heavy moan.

"Fuuuck, Jaxsen. I need you here right now." She rolls her head back onto her pillow before lifting her gaze to meet mine.

I'm transfixed on her before I snap out of it, quickly unbuttoning my pants and shove them to the floor with my boxer briefs. My dick springs in attention, and her eyes zero in on my hard length. I wrap my tight fist around my dick, giving it a slow pump.

"Let me see you play with that sweet pussy, Emmy."

She nods, obeying my order, and moves to sit on her knees pushing her shorts down and kicking them off the side of the bed. She lies back, bending her arm behind her head, and spreads her legs open for me giving me a perfect view of her pussy.

She trails her hand back down her chest, over her stomach, down her inner thigh, and back up the other side before she brushes over her clit. Her eyes never leave mine, watching as I eat up every inch of her. When she slips her fingers inside, her back arches off the bed before moving back to rub her clit, tilting her head back in pleasure.

"Jaxsen," she moans. "I don't think I'm gonna last long."

"Let me watch you use your toy, Emmy. Spread that pussy open and cum for me, baby."

She sits up, reaches for her vibrator, and flicks it back on. She slowly moves the toy over her stomach, following the same path her hand did before she presses it against her clit.

I spit on my hand, roughly sliding my hand up and down my hard dick.

Her body trembles and her legs quiver, releasing a breathy groan, mixed with the muffled sound of my name. She taps the vibrator against her clit, pulling back to reveal her glistening pussy.

"Fuck, baby, you're so wet for me."

"Jaxsen," she heaves. "Help me cum."

God damn, I wish I was there devouring every inch of her.

"Close your eyes, baby." She nods, leaning her head back. "Imagine I'm with you, flicking my tongue over your tight clit, licking and sucking it into my mouth."

"Mmm," she moans. "It feels so fuckin' good."

"You taste so good, baby. You look so fuckin' sexy with your legs wrapped around my head."

"Jaxsen," she breathes out harshly.

"I want to feel your pussy tighten around me. I'm running the tip of my dick over your clit and down to your pussy, sliding into your tight cunt."

She sucks in a deep breath at my choice of words, clenching her thighs around her arm.

"Damn, you look so good taking my dick. You're so tight, so hot around me."

My fist tightens around my cock. I screw my eyes shut, envisioning her warm pussy clenching around me.

"Your tits look beautiful bouncing for me as I fuck you hard and fast. I'm close baby," I grunt, pumping my dick harder.

"I'm leaning over to lick and suck your nipples into my mouth.

"Oh my God," she moans, her legs falling open.

She taps the vibrator against her pussy again when her body starts trembling, and she throws her head back again, arching off the bed before she slams her legs shut around her vibrator.

"I'm coming, Jaxsen." She huffs out before clamping her mouth shut.

The sight of her body trembling with the force of her release has hot ribbons of semen shooting over my hand and chest.

She's fuckin' perfect.

"I swear, baby, you were made for me."

CHAPTER FIFTEEN

EMMY

Jaxsen is standing near the SUV when I step outside and jog down the stairs. It feels like it's been so long since I've seen him. I'm practically sprinting toward him when I run and jump into his arms.

Greg is standing behind him, chuckling, when Jaxsen holds out his arms, ready to catch me.

"Hi Greg," I sing, my arms and legs wrapped around Jaxsen.

"Ms. Kincaid." He nods toward me. "Nice to see you."

"You, too." I smile, pulling back to stare down at Jaxsen.

He's wearing the biggest smile I've ever seen on his face. I hold his face in my hands, feeling the rough stubble beneath my palms before I kiss him.

Hard and full of passion, making up for every second we've been apart.

I don't know how things seemed to progress between us so fast, but he's quickly become one of the most important people in my life.

When we're not together, I'm thinking about him. We've survived the last couple weeks by texting and FaceTiming as often as we can. I was so used to being away from Matthew when we were together, as both of our jobs had us working out of town. Despite being together for almost three years, I never felt as close to him or missed him as much as I have being away from Jaxsen.

I think it says a lot about the difference between the two relationships.

Time and distance mean nothing when someone means so much to you.

Jaxsen makes an effort, even when we're apart, to make me feel special and to let me know he's thinking of me. Whether it's a good morning message, sending flowers with a note saying he misses me, or even ordering dinner to be delivered one night so we could eat together.

It's not about the money or what he gives me, but the intention behind everything he does.

I guess when you've been mistreated in the past, you come to appreciate the little things.

"Hi baby," he murmurs when he pulls back.

"Hello to you." I rub my lips together, feeling them tingle from his kiss, attempting to cover up the smile threatening to break across my face.

He lowers me to the ground, and I take a step back, getting a good look at him. He looks delicious in his black joggers and T-shirt. The material is thin for the warm summer air of Miami, enough to outline the front of his pants.

My eyes stop before darting back up to look at him.

"What?" he asks, raising a questioning brow.

"Nothing," I quip.

Doesn't he have any idea how dangerous sweatpants are to women?

I step past him, brushing my hand over the front of his pants. He sucks in a deep breath as I climb into the back passenger seat.

His eyes blaze with desire when I cast him a knowing look. He leans over me, reaching for the belt buckle, and I smirk.

"Want me to take care of that for you?" I grin, implying the double meaning.

He pulls back from me and shakes his head. "Like hell you will."

"Is that right, Mr. Wild?"

"If you're with me, Ms. Kincaid," he says, enunciating each syllable. "I will always be the one to take care of you."

He leans in closer, sucking all the oxygen from the space. His eyes are bright with purpose, challenging me to test him.

"Okay," I say, giving in.

"Okay?" he questions as if he expected me to fight him on it.

I nod. "Okay."

"That's all you got for me. Just *okay*."

I look past him, seeing Greg standing a few feet behind him. He's poised, his back straight and his arms crossed in front of him in a military stance. He doesn't move, doesn't say a word, but I know he hears us.

I lean in close, pressing my mouth to Jaxsen's ear, letting my warm breath feather over his skin, earning me a heavy exhale.

"You've always been very good at taking care of me," I whisper breathlessly. "So yes, just *okay*."

He clenches his jaw, adjusting the seatbelt across my body. This time when he moves the strap over me, he runs his hand over my breast, forcing me to inhale sharply.

"Quit teasing me," I mutter, the words coming out needy.

I clench my thighs together, and he glances down, watching me.

"Or what?"

"I haven't been able to touch you in six days." My voice drops low. "Not like I want to, anyway. Don't make me wait any longer by teasing you back."

His eyes narrow on my lips before locking with mine as if debating whether he wants to push me more or give in. He must settle the debate in his mind when his mouth crashes down on mine.

I reach my hands up to hold his face, only this time, when I feel his tongue brush against my lips, I open up for him.

"Jesus Christ!" He grunts, his chest heaving when he leans back. "What the hell are you doing to me?"

"And to think I'm only getting started." I smirk.

I don't miss how he subtly tries to adjust himself, covering his hard-on when the door shuts behind him and he rounds the back of the SUV. He climbs in and slides all the way over again, his leg touching mine. His large hand covers my thigh in a possessive move. His fingers brush against the seam between my legs, all while keeping his eyes faced forward, driving me crazy.

"I will get you back for this," I whisper, looking over at Greg in the rearview mirror.

If he hears me, he doesn't give any sign on his face. He's stoic and focused, his hands on the wheel as the city speeds past us.

Jaxsen's lips curl on the side and I shake my head in frustration.

"What are we doing tonight?" I ask, attempting to change the subject.

We hadn't talked about what our plans were. All I know is we haven't been together in almost a week, and all I care about is spending time with him.

When his flight landed, he messaged me he was en route and to be ready.

"I was hoping you wouldn't mind another quiet night in." He turns his head toward me to gauge my response.

He told me to dress casually in something comfortable, so I figured we weren't planning on going out. I don't mind at all. I was able to get someone to cover my shift at the airline so we could spend the weekend together.

We've both been nonstop go, go, go since I started my internship. I desperately needed and wanted a quiet weekend, just the two of us.

"I have practice in the morning, so I was thinking we could get dinner and go back to my place, maybe watch a movie. Would that be okay?"

"Sounds perfect." I smile, tilting my head up and press a kiss against his lips.

He looks deep in thought when I pull back, and for a second, I wonder if something is bothering him.

"Can I cook for you?" I ask.

"If you want to, you can. My housekeeper stopped by the store a couple days ago, so we should have enough to find something to make."

My mind gets lost in thought about the people in his life.

A driver and security, an assistant, and now a house-keeper. Who else does he have working for him?

Our lives are so vastly different.

"How'd you get into playing basketball?"

We've talked about his time in college and when he got drafted into the NBA, but not about where it all started. When you're left to phone and video calls to keep in touch, you do a lot more talking and getting to know each other.

He's shared with me his relationship with his mom and how she raised him as a single parent. He's the only child. Despite taking care of him on her own, she busted her ass to keep him in every basketball program he could be in.

"Two of my best friends from elementary school are brothers and loved playing basketball, although their home lives were different than mine. I guess you could say they weren't given the same opportunities I was."

My mind goes back to the night of the charity event and his passion for helping underprivileged and homeless kids. I can't help but feel like it has something to do with this story, and I'm about to peel back another layer to Jaxsen Wild, showing me he's the opposite of the man the media makes him out to be.

"Despite everything, though, we stuck together and played through high school. When our team made it to state and won, offers from all over started pouring in. Scholarships and full rides, I had my pick at the top three schools in the nation. Darius and Damien, though, it wasn't the same for them. It was frustrating as hell to see two of my best friends, who I watched day in and day out, bust their asses and work hard, so full of talent and passion, be looked over."

I turn my face back toward the front and catch Greg's eyes in the mirror.

We all suspected the same reason why they were overlooked without having to acknowledge it out loud.

"Is that why you stayed in Georgia to play?"

He nods. "I wanted to play with Darius. Damien ended up going a different route and decided to focus on school, getting his degree in computer science. He's a total computer whiz, but Darius, he loved the game as much as I do, if not more."

My heart seizes in my chest, thinking about him choosing a different route out of his loyalty to playing with his best friend.

"What happened to him after college?"

"He made it to the NBA. He was drafted by San Antonio. He played for them for two years before he got injured. He went up for a contested dunk and twisted his back, landing on it wrong when he came down. He's had five different surgeries, but he chose to retire early."

"Wow, that's terrible."

To think of all he'd gone through to do what he loved, to make it through every adversity and obstacle put in his way, only to have it all taken away, is heartbreaking.

Jaxsen's hand squeezes my thigh and I stare out the window, replaying the story in my mind.

"Is that why you founded Be Wild? To help other kids like Darius and Damien go after their dreams?"

He doesn't have enough time to respond before Greg pipes up.

"Like I said, Ms. Emmy, Hollywood Tea will have you thinking he's a loose cannon, but Jaxsen's a better man than people know."

"Don't lie to her, G. Certainly, if it's published on Hollywood Tea, it has to be the truth."

They both laugh and I roll my eyes. I reach up and turn his face to look back at me.

"You can't fool me, Jaxsen. There's not a single bad thing they could print about you that I'd believe."

His smile falls and his eyes soften. He reaches out and brushes his thumb over my bottom lip.

"You should," he whispers. "I haven't always been a good guy, ya know."

"Don't lie to me, Jaxsen."

Narrowing his gaze on me, he leans in and kisses me. I slide my fingers over his forearm, gripping his wrists in my hands, holding on for the ride. His forehead presses against mine when he breaks the kiss.

"I've made mistakes and hurt people I cared about ..." His voice trails off.

"We all have a past, Jaxsen. That doesn't mean it has to dictate our future."

"You make me want to be a better person than I've been."

"And I'll be there, every step of the way."

He exhales heavily, almost as if he's sighing in relief.

"What I did to deserve you, I'll never know, but I don't want to lose you."

"You won't," I reassure him. "You promised to take care of me, remember?"

"Damn right, I did." He grins, his voice dropping low. "Wait until we get back to my place. I'll take care of you on every surface in my apartment."

"Quit teasing me, Mr. Wild, and do it already."

CHAPTER SIXTEEN

EMMY

"Jaxsen tells me you two met when he was in New York."

When Jaxsen told me he got tickets to take me to the game, I didn't realize it meant we'd be sitting next to his mom, Sonya, too.

She turns to look at me, her smile beaming at the thought of how we met.

It's halftime, and Miami is up by five points. We used the intermission to run up to the concessions to grab a snack. When I came back to our seat with a pickle on a stick, Kaylee lost her mind.

"We did," I reply, holding a napkin over my mouth to dab the juices from my lips. "He was a passenger on my flight when we flew back to Miami."

It's the truth. I'm just leaving out the part about how we got delayed, ended up running into each other at the hotel bar, and hooking up.

"How can she take you seriously with that damn thing in your mouth?" Kaylee mutters under her breath, as I take another bite.

I narrow my eyes at her, silently telling her to shut it.

As soon as I saw the sign advertising them, I knew I couldn't pass up the chance to get one. Pickles were one of my favorite snacks back at school, although it's been forever since I've had one.

"I didn't have any idea who he was, though," I say, turning my attention back to Sonya. "It wasn't until Kaylee told me when we were fitting him for his suit that I found out."

She smiles, clearly liking my answer.

I wonder if she met Kelly or any of Jaxsen's other girlfriends.

The buzzer rings and the players start jogging out of the locker room and onto the court. Jaxsen makes a beeline toward where we're sitting courtside. He flashes me a wink, leaning in and kissing his mom on the cheek before doing the same to me. He presses his mouth to my ear and mumbles, "I'm not going to be able to focus if I look over at you eating that damn thing while wearing my number."

Kaylee nearly chokes next to me, evidently overhearing him.

"I tried to warn her," she jokes.

Jaxsen pulls back, blowing me a kiss and waving at Kaylee before taking off across the court.

"Good grief, the way he looks at you. I swear, you're gonna end up pregnant with one wink."

I swat her thigh to hush her. "Will you shut up?"

I glance around, wondering if anyone overheard. The last thing we need are rumors going around.

"What? What if you are already? I mean, look at you, you're eating a damn pickle."

"No, I'm not," I grit my teeth, trying to keep my voice low.

Sonya's too focused on watching Jaxsen warm up to hear anything we're saying, which is a good thing. My mind is swirling with thoughts, imagining the scenario she just planted in my head.

Pregnant? I couldn't possibly be pregnant, could I?

I quickly pull out my phone and scroll through the app where I keep track of my periods. They've been irregular my entire life. My mom got me on birth control early to help with regulating them because the pain was unbearable.

Even when it does come, it's only some light spotting for a day or two.

I've been so distracted between school and work, then work and the internship, I lost track of the last time I had one.

It doesn't mean I'm pregnant, though.

I start replaying memories of the last few weeks, piecing together any possible signs or symptoms. Eating a pickle on a stick could hardly count as a sign, which is crazy for her to insinuate off that fact alone.

Until the memories of me dizzy on one of the flights with Cody rings clear in my mind, or how surprised I was when the dress for the gala didn't fit.

Or how run-down and tired I've felt lately.

I've been a mess of emotions too.

Shit.

The buzzer sounds again, signaling the start of the third quarter. The players run to the center of the court for tip-off.

Jaxsen and another player go up for the ball, knocking it to one of the Chicago players.

"De-fense! De-fense! De-fense!"

The crowd around us starts to erupt, chanting in unison to cheer the Blaze on. The rest of the game has me on pins and needles. Despite playing hard, Miami lost, making it one-to-one in the series. It's going to be a tough loss for Jaxsen, especially playing in front of their home crowd and his mom.

After the game wraps up, I'm waiting outside the locker room with Sonya for Jaxsen. I planned on staying with Jaxsen tonight, so Kaylee took off for home.

"I'm gonna run to the restroom quick. Tell Jaxsen to wait for me when he comes out, okay?" She pats me on the arm, flashing me a warm smile.

I nod, and she takes off toward the line forming in the lobby for the bathroom.

Jaxsen normally showers after his game, so it could be a bit before he comes out anyway.

I notice a man dressed in a charcoal gray suit and black shoes standing across from me, leaning against the wall, his legs crossed in front of him. His hair is slicked back, oozing an arrogance that makes your lip curl.

It's loud in here, with people gathering around the fan shop to buy merch and memorabilia.

He must sense my eyes on him; he glances up and narrows his gaze at me. The look in his eyes is cold and calculated.

I adjust my stance, leaning my shoulder against the wall, pulling out my phone from my purse to distract myself. I have a missed call from my mom and several unread messages from Cody telling me about a date he had tonight.

I open the text, scrolling through his messages, and fire off a response.

When I glance up, I notice the man is still looking over at me before quickly turning back to his phone. His jaw is clenched, his throat bobbing when he swallows hard. His agitation is evident in his features.

Either he knows who I am, or he's pissed at me for looking at him.

Minutes tick by before Jaxsen steps out of the locker room, sauntering toward me. He wraps his arms around me in a warm hug. He stands over a foot taller than me, hiding me from the rest of the room when he leans in to kiss me.

"Hey, baby," he whispers. "I gotta talk to the press for a quick interview. Will you wait for me?"

I nod. "Your mom wants to see you too, but she ran to the bathroom."

Jaxsen notices the man from a moment ago standing behind him, nodding his head in greeting.

"Okay, I'll be quick. You can stay here, or I can have Adrian bring you back when she gets done in the bathroom."

I furrow my brows, trying to figure out how he knows him.

"He's my manager," he answers, reading my mind.

Evidently, he does know who I am, or why else would he look at me the way he did?

If looks could kill, I'd be dead on the spot.

"I'll stay here until your mom comes back. Give us a few more minutes, and she should be back."

He nods, squeezing my hand and winks before he crosses the room to talk to Adrian. He leans in close, motioning with his hands toward the hallway before pointing over his shoulder to me.

Jaxsen claps him on the back, turns to wave at me, then disappears down the long corridor. I flash a hesitant smile at Adrian, hoping to smooth over whatever awkward introduction we just had before searching for any sign of Sonya.

"So, you're the Emmy he's been talking all about."

A deep voice grumbles from beside me, sending my head turning back to find him standing in front of me.

I get a waft of his cologne. It's heavy, smelling of citrus and cloves. It reminds me of Matthew. It's strong, with an air of pretentiousness oozing from him.

Who does this guy think he is?

"That would be me," I retort, wanting to roll my eyes.

He narrows his, looking for any sign to test my strength, but I'd be damned if I'd let this man make me wither away.

Not now, not in this lifetime.

His eyes rake over my body, doing a quick once over. It's calculated as if he's trying to read beneath the surface to gauge my intentions with Jaxsen.

If he thinks I'm someone he needs to worry about or he's going to scare away, he's wrong. I want what's best for Jaxsen, probably more than he does, with the way he stalks over here trying to intimidate me.

"As I'm sure you're aware, Jaxsen has a lot riding on this season. It should come as no surprise to you that he doesn't need any distractions right now. Not with everything on the line with the championship, his contract, hell, his career. Do me a favor, stay out of his way and, even better, out of mine."

I grit my teeth. Get in his way?

I curl my lip in a smirk. This time, I don't bother holding back the urge to roll my eyes, returning his dirty look with one of my own.

He clenches his jaw, not appreciating the change in my demeanor.

I'll be polite and respectful to anyone, but the second you step out of line, I'll be the first one to remind you where the hell your place is.

"I'm guessing your little spiel has worked at chasing away women in the past. You must think you're dealing with someone who you can run over with your bullshit."

He tilts his chin in defiance.

"If you're protecting him, I understand, but you don't need to protect him from me. I hate to break it to you, though, but I'm not going anywhere, and I most certainly won't wilt away like a delicate flower at your condescending threats. Something tells me if Jaxsen found out the way you were speaking to me, he wouldn't be very happy either."

He rolls his jaw, not liking the idea of me bringing up Jaxsen finding out about his attempt to warn me away. We both know he'd be livid if he did.

I chuckle. "That's what I thought."

I notice Sonya approaching in the corner of my eye, but I keep my gaze focused on Adrian.

"I guess what I'm trying to say is, stay out of our relationship and we won't have a problem. Do I make myself clear?"

He turns, attempting to end the conversation when I repeat myself, this time my voice sterner than before.

"Do I make myself clear?"

He nods and turns to look at me, fire blazing in his eyes.

He's ticked, but he'll never say it because he knows he stepped out of line. This is his one and only warning.

I won't let him or anyone else come between our relationship. I may not know much about this life, but I won't cower away at the first sign of trouble either.

I've always been the one who put more into my relationships, made sacrifices in an attempt to prove my love, and fought to keep us together. It's different with Jaxsen, though.

He's never given me a reason to question where he stands, and I won't let him forget what he means to me.

"Good, now if you will, please take us to Jaxsen's press conference," I say, smiling as Sonya links her arm with mine.

Adrian notices her standing next to me, his eyes falling back on me before holding his arm out to lead the way.

"Nice to see you again, Adrian." Sonya smiles. "Thank you for showing us the way.

"Yes, Adrian," I say, my voice serious. "Thank you."

CHAPTER SEVENTEEN

EMMY

I release a heavy sigh, brace my hands on the edge of the bathroom vanity, and squeeze my eyes shut.

Ever since Kaylee's comment about possibly being pregnant, it's all I've been able to think about.

What if I'm pregnant?

My mind keeps replaying all the signs over the past few weeks, back to the night we spent together at the hotel.

My stomach rolls at the thought and I fall to the floor, pulling my legs against my chest and resting my forehead against my knees.

I'm not in any place to be having a kid. We just started seeing each other and haven't officially come out as being in a relationship. What if he thinks I'm doing this to trap him?

If anyone were to speculate who I am to him, all the rumors would be put to rest with the way he kissed me the night of the gala, like he was ready to drag me back to his bedroom.

My lips tingle and my mouth curves at the memory.

I've never felt this way with anyone my whole life. As much as I'm scared of what the results could be, there's an excitement fluttering in my stomach at the thought of having a baby.

Not because I want to push things quickly, but the thought of sharing a baby makes my heart seize. Someone who's half me and half him.

Now may not be the right time, though. We haven't had a chance to enjoy the early stages of our relationship without the chaos of the season and my internship going on. There's still so much I want to do: travel, finish school, buy a home, settle down, and get married.

I glance up at the counter to the test left waiting for me. I reach my hands out and pull myself up, deciding there's no better way to put my worries and fears to rest than getting it over with and finding out now.

I fumble while my shaking hands open the box before dropping the packaged stick onto the counter. Flipping the box over, I read the instructions before ripping the test open.

"What am I doing?" I mutter to myself.

My eyes scan over the directions before moving to sit on the toilet. I've been drinking more water lately after the whole dizzy spell. Cody insisted it's because I haven't been taking care of myself. He's constantly on me now. I swear, he hounds me like a mother hen, but I know it's because he loves me and is looking out for me.

I uncap the test and quickly take care of business before putting the cap back on and setting it on the counter.

The test says you must wait five minutes, and it's the most excruciatingly long five minutes of my life.

I wash my hands before splashing water on my face. Jaxsen is away at his game in Chicago; it starts in a couple hours. I decide no matter what the test says, I'm going to spend the rest of the night enjoying some self-care and park it on the couch while I watch him play.

"Whatever the results are, it's going to be okay," I reassure myself. "It's all going to be okay."

I nod, mustering up the courage to pick up the test and release a heavy sigh. I opted for one of the foolproof ones that displays the words on the screen, so I'll know without a shadow of a doubt.

I flip it over to read it, my heart seizing in my chest as tears fill the brim of my eyes.

PREGNANT.

"Oh God," I murmur, squeezing my eyes shut.

I know this isn't the end of the world like I'm making it out to be, but it isn't at all how I envisioned this happening. I can't help but wonder how Jaxsen will react—if he'll be upset or as scared as I am right now.

I'm a ball of anxiety for the rest of the evening. To help me relax, I run a bath, adding some candles and a lavender bath bomb. Kaylee is out for the night with some girlfriends, and I'm thankful I have the space to myself to collect my thoughts.

After my bath, I put on some silk pajamas and tie my hair up into a bun before I crawl into bed and flip on the TV to watch the pregame show. My phone vibrates on my nightstand, and I mute the sound, smiling when I see the name Momma flash on the screen.

I swipe the screen to answer, "Hi, Mom."

"Hi, sweetheart," she croons. "It's the strangest thing. I got this weird feeling something was wrong, and I wanted to call and see how my baby girl is doing."

Tears prick my eyes. My mom has been there for me through everything. Even when the breakup with Matthew happened, she was there next to me, wiping away my tears, reminding me not to give up on love.

She was never a big fan of him. Although she saw the red flags before I was willing to acknowledge them. Even despite that, though, she was always supportive of me and our relationship, letting me make decisions for myself and trusting I would do what was best for me.

"I'm glad you called," I say. We haven't had a chance to catch up lately.

I told her about my relationship with Jaxsen the last time we chatted the day after his basketball game when I met Sonya. She could sense something changed in me, picking up the happier note in my voice.

"Is everything okay?"

"Yeah," I force out, hoping it's more convincing than it sounds in my head. "A lot going on, but that's to be expected. Right?"

She sighs. "You've always been one to like having a full plate. I hate to say it, but I think you thrive in chaos. Not me, though, we've always been opposites in that way."

Ain't that the truth.

I grew up very similar to Jaxsen, living in a single-parent household. My dad bailed when I was younger, and my mom struggled raising me and my sister, Alexa, but she always did what she had to do to put food on the table and clothes on our backs.

I was always on the go, wanting to do a hundred things in one day. Whereas she was the opposite. She's enjoyed the simple things in life and didn't like to get bogged down with the constant running around.

She did, though, for me and Alexa. She's always been supportive, scraping every penny together if it meant giving us the things we wanted.

I still remember when she bought me my first sewing machine. She had just lost her job, and it was less than two weeks before Christmas, but it didn't stop her from doing everything she could to make it magical for us.

I remember how guilty I felt when I saw her old record player disappear from our living room. She spent weeks convincing me it was broken and she had to get rid of it, but I always suspected she sold it to make some extra cash.

Her record player meant everything to her. She loved listening to old records of Johnny Cash and Loretta Lynn while she made me breakfast in the morning before school.

I adjust the pillow behind my head, pulling my covers up to my chest, catching up with her about life. She doesn't know it, but I need this chat more than anything right now.

Something about talking to her, thinking about her strength in raising us, reminded me everything was going to be okay.

If she could raise two kids on her own, I know I can do this too. I still can't help but be thankful, trusting that Jaxsen will be there for our baby.

He's loyal to the people he cares about, and I know he'll love our baby, even if we choose to go our separate ways.

He wouldn't walk away from our child.

When the game is about to start, I let my mom go with the promise of video calling her later this week to eat breakfast together before work.

The game tips off and I can hear the crowd in the arena cheering on Chicago. This is a big game tonight. Miami is up three-to-two, and if they win tonight, they are going to the finals.

One more win and Jaxsen's one step closer to the championship.

My stomach is in knots watching the game. At one point, Jaxsen goes up for a shot and a defender leaps out of nowhere and bats the ball away, sending him crashing to the floor.

Immediately, my mind is on the story he told me about Darius, fear pumping through me when he jumps back to his feet, wincing as he massages his fingers into his hip bone before waving over at Coach Carr, reassuring him he's okay.

I sag in relief, not wanting to think about him getting injured when he's come this far and is so close to winning.

They are neck and neck the entire game. Every time they get a little bit of a lead, Chicago comes in guns blazing and strikes back.

"C'mon, Jaxsen! C'mon!" I chant at the TV.

I'd never watched a basketball game until the night Kaylee invited me to go with her; now, here I am, sitting at home alone, watching my boyfriend slash baby daddy.

What has my life become?

The clock runs down to below two minutes, and Chicago is up 92-87.

I don't know if the nausea rolling through me is from my anxiety or pregnancy sickness. Miami calls a timeout and I leap out of bed, pacing back and forth around my small room.

The Blaze have the ball, and Jaxsen throws it in from out of bounds, bouncing it toward Miles. I recognize his name as one of Jaxsen's close friends.

The clock continues to tick down when he passes the ball to Rush, who dribbles it between his legs before taking a step back and throwing up a shot.

The player guarding him jumps at the same time, knocking Jaxsen on the arm.

I slap my hand over my mouth, attempting to cover up the sound of my scream, when he makes the shot with a swish of the net. The whistle is blown, and I frantically throw my hands up.

"Oh my God, what the heck is happening?" I shout. "Someone, please explain what's going on."

The commentator, as if speaking directly to me, follows it up calling it a critical foul and a costly move on Chicago, sending Colson to the line.

Miami is only down by one point now.

"These are mistakes you simply cannot make if you're Chicago, giving the best scorer in the league another chance to make a shot with the conference championship on the line," the announcer says.

I watch in anticipation while clapping my hands and bouncing on my feet.

Colson steps up to the free-throw line, wipes his hands on his shorts, and bounces the ball. His face is blank, concentration marking his features.

The ball goes up, and I swear, the only sound I hear is my adrenaline rushing through me. I hold my breath, waiting for the ball to land, and it sinks perfectly into the net.

"Yes, yes! Oh my God, yes!"

With twenty-three seconds left of the game, they are tied, and Chicago has the ball.

My anxiety is riding high watching the last few seconds of the game tick down. When Crew goes up for a shot, Jaxsen is on him like a second skin. As soon as the ball is in the air, Jaxsen swats it away, and Colson is right behind him, chasing after the ball.

It all happens so quickly as they race down the court. When he bounces the ball back to Jaxsen, Jaxsen goes up for the shot just as the buzzer hits.

Everything moves in slow motion when the ball bounces against the rim before going in.

"They won! Jaxsen won!" I fall to my knees, clapping enthusiastically.

I tilt my head back, staring up at the ceiling with tears streaming down my face.

This must be the hormones hitting me, but I'm so happy I can barely hold myself together.

They won.

CHAPTER EIGHTEEN

JAXSEN

Miles: Bro, you need to check Hollywood Tea.

I pull up outside the practice gym and put my car in park. Miles's text message flashes over the screen on my dashboard. I pick up my phone, open the message, and the link to an article immediately follows.

I don't even have a chance to read the headline when a familiar picture appears on my screen, and my heart sinks.

Leaked Photos of Jaxsen Wild with unidentified woman hit the internet

Photos reportedly have surfaced on the internet showing a nude Jaxsen Wild, point guard with the Miami Blaze, with an unidentified woman. Many speculate the woman in the photographs is Kelly Eaton, who was rumored as dating Wild last year. Kelly Eaton is now dating Crew Savage, longtime rival of Jaxsen Wild, who plays for Chicago.

What could this mean for Wild and his focus heading into the NBA Finals? With the Championship on the line, will he be able to tune out the noise and keep his head in the game?

We've reached out to reps for Jaxsen Wild and, so far, no word.

The article says it was posted two hours ago. As soon as I woke up, I checked my phone for messages from Emmy before taking off to practice. We flew in late last night. She was already asleep when we landed, so I ended up going straight home.

I scroll through my contacts and aggressively tap Adrian's name, lifting my phone to my ear.

"I'm on it," he answers, skipping a greeting.

"We knew something like this would happen. Crew wasn't going to let me roll on past Chicago without making me pay for it."

"I don't know if Crew is behind this, Jaxsen."

"What do you mean you don't know if it's Crew? Of course, it is! The woman in the fuckin' photo is his girlfriend, Adrian. You have to be an idiot to think he's not involved."

"What does he gain if these photos are released?"

I squeeze the phone in my hand, wanting to shake the life out of him. What doesn't he get about this? It's not about me with his girlfriend.

"It's no secret there's bad blood between us. There's no way in hell he's gonna sit back and watch me beat his team, make it to the finals, and win a championship. It's all a game to him, man. He's trying to get in my head, distract me, and steer my focus off track."

My phone vibrates in my hand again. I pull back to check the screen and see a message roll through from Emmy saying she'll be over after practice.

Fuck.

"I promise, man. I'll find out who's responsible for the photos and make them pay for it."

"It doesn't matter now, Adrian. They're out there. I need to know whoever it was won't be doing this shit again."

I hit end and slouch against the seat. I massage my fingers over my eyes, needing to pull myself together and get through practice.

How am I going to explain this to Emmy?

I don't know if she's heard the news and, although I wish I could tell her in person, the last thing I want is for her to find out by reading the article.

Me: Rumors are going around about me, pictures circulating the internet from before we met. Please, do me a favor, just avoid reading about it until we have a chance to talk in person.

A part of me is worried this will be too much for her, and it'll end up pushing her away.

I can't help but feel like Kelly is the mastermind, but I still believe Crew is behind it, too. She was pissed off and jealous the night of the gala. After we left, she blew up my phone to the point I ended up blocking her number.

It doesn't strike me as surprising that the day after we beat Chicago, photos from when we were together are leaked, and she's the only other person who would've had access to them.

She's trying to drive a wedge between me and Emmy in hopes it'll push her away.

After what happened with her ex, I wouldn't blame her if she decided this was too much for her and she wanted to bow out. My heart aches at the thought of her walking away from me.

We still haven't came out publicly as being together, and when things began, she wasn't looking for a relationship.

She gave me the wrong number, for fuck's sake.

I power off my phone and shove it into my bag, not wanting or needing any other distractions right now. Whatever happens will have to wait until after.

I'm drenched in sweat after practice, but thankfully they took it easy on us. We have our first game against Los Angeles tomorrow night and want us to try and conserve our energy.

I hit the shower, and we all grab a light dinner while we watch footage from the last time we played L.A.

They are going to be a tough team for us to beat. Defensively, they're damn near unstoppable. I'm trying not to think about anything but the game in front of us or let the outside noise distract me.

One game at a time.

I swing by Coach's office on my way out, adjusting my gym bag on my shoulder before I hit two knocks on the doorframe.

"You got a minute?" I ask, peering my head in.

Colson is sitting in the chair across from him.

He nods. "We were just wrapping up actually."

I clap Rush on the back, giving him a quick hug. He mutters under his breath about not letting the rumors get into my head and to call him if I need to chat.

He's always been there when I need him.

"How's everything going? How are you handling this?" Coach asks, sitting back in his chair, crossing his arms over his chest.

I drop my bag on the floor and fall back into the chair, running my hand over my forehead and temples.

"Doin' my best to tune it out, but you know how it is. It's not easy to do, especially this far into the season with everything on the line."

He narrows his eyes and nods.

"What about Emmy? How are things with her?"

I shake my head and shrug, not sure how to respond. Things have been great between us, but who knows what will happen after this.

"We've both been working a lot. I haven't had the chance to talk to her, but she's coming over to my place in a bit."

"How long have you two been seeing each other?"

His questions throw me off. Where is he going with this? Does he think she's behind the photos?

"A couple months. We met on my flight back from NYC after the suspension."

His eyes widen in understanding.

"What's that look for?" I chuckle.

"You seem different lately. More controlled, focused. The old Jaxsen would've been losing his temper, feeding into the drama. It's something we wouldn't need right now this far into the playoffs, but you're different. It makes me wonder if she isn't why."

I hadn't thought much about it. I already got my verbal lashing back in New York. The last thing I needed was to make matters worse.

My contract is still up for renewal this fall, and there's a lot riding on the next few games.

Emmy has calmed me in a lot of ways. Not only could I risk losing everything I've worked hard for, but I could be throwing away what I have with her, too, if I let shit get to me.

"I guess I hadn't thought about it that way. I'm getting older, and I'm sick of the drama, ya know? I've had a taste of what a healthy relationship is like with her, and I don't have any interest in stirring shit up anymore."

Coach smiles and nods. "That's what I like to hear, son."

Someone knocks on the door, and I turn to find Miles peering his head in. "Uhh, sorry to interrupt, but Jaxsen, I think you should check your phone."

My heart sinks, immediately fearing what it could be.

"Another article went up."

My face drops, and I sag against the chair. I turn back toward Coach, running my hand over my face.

"I can't prove it, Coach, but I swear to you, I think Savage is behind all this."

"What do you mean?"

"Those photos, they are of me, but the woman in them is his girlfriend. We were together—"

He nods, holding his hand up to stop me, knowing where this is going.

I unzip the side pocket on my bag and pull out my phone, turning it back on. A whole slew of messages come through, causing my phone to vibrate repeatedly.

"Jesus," Miles mutters under his breath, seeing all the messages come through one after another.

I notice a text from Adrian asking me to call him, followed by a link to another article.

God, when will it stop?

My heart is practically beating out of my chest waiting for the article to load. A picture of me with Emmy at the charity gala appears, followed by an old one of me in a heated conversation with Kelly.

Jaxsen Wild photographed with newest fling the same night he's rumored to have spent the evening with his ex, Kelly Eaton.

"Are you fuckin' kidding me?"

To anyone looking at the article, I can see where they could believe the lies they're spewing, but it's not at all how it looks.

Another message comes through from Emmy, letting me know she'll meet me at my place in about thirty minutes.

I have no idea if Emmy has seen these articles, but if she has, there's no telling what she'll think when she does.

"Emmy is on her way to my place. I have to get going." I shake my head.

"Coach, I know this is creating a distraction right now, one that's not needed for you and the team. I swear, I'd bet money Savage is behind this, stirring things up because he's pissed we beat Chicago. It doesn't matter, though, because I'm not going to let it affect me. I need to be with Emmy right now, but come tomorrow when we play L.A., you have my word my focus will be on winning that game."

He nods and stands. "If you need anything, give me a call."

I shake his hand and storm out of the practice gym, making a beeline for my car. Reporters are waiting outside, and I silently regret not having Greg bring me this morning.

I want to make whoever is behind this pay for it. If I lose Emmy, I will see to it that they do.

Come hell or high water.

CHAPTER NINETEEN

JAXSEN

I'm standing in the living room gritting my teeth, listening to Adrian rattle on about doing damage control when a soft knock hits my door.

Emmy.

There's no one else it could be, and my body relaxes at the thought of her finally being here.

Nude photos of me have been leaked. Hollywood Tea is once again dragging my name through the mud, insinuating I've been messing around behind her back. I don't care what they say about me. I've dealt with it enough throughout my career, but it's Emmy they are messing with now.

She's tied to me, and I hate the thought of her being dragged into this and them tainting what we have.

I open the door and she's standing in front of me. She's dressed in denim shorts, a yellow flowy tank top, and a pair of white sandals.

My eyes follow the path down her body, stopping on her bright pink toes before making my way back up to meet her eyes. She left her hair down, and it's falling in waves down her back.

I'm half tempted to hang up on Adrian and pull her into my bedroom. She bites her lip to fight off her grin, loving how my eyes are on fire for her.

"Hi, handsome." She grins.

"Hi, baby," I mouth, holding my phone to my ear. Adrian is still going on and on, and I've lost track of what he's talking about. I've tuned him out. I can't find it in me to care anymore.

I reach for her hand, and she follows me inside.

"Hey, Adrian," I interrupt him, and he goes silent. "Something came up. I gotta go. I won't be around for the rest of the night. Can you just email me?"

He fumbles for a second before saying yes.

I don't bother waiting for him to respond further before I end the call, turn my phone on silent and toss it absentmindedly on the couch.

"I've missed you," I whisper, pulling her into my arms.

"I've missed you." She sighs, and I can't help but wonder if there's something more to that sigh. There's so much we need to talk about, but it's been days since I've last seen her, and it's felt more like years with everything going on.

She runs her finger over my chest, tilting her head back to stare up at me.

I lean into her and press a soft kiss against her lips, bending down to grip her thighs and lift her into my arms.

I'm afraid to admit this out loud, but a part of me is worried about what will happen if this gets to be too much for her.

She drops her purse on the floor and kicks off her shoes. She tangles her arms around my neck, crashing her lips against mine.

I don't want to think about everything right now. I just want to be closer to her. I need to feel her skin against mine.

I carry her through my apartment, down the hall toward my bedroom. She trails a line of kisses from my lips, over my cheek, and down my neck. She pulls back, her cheeks flushed and grinds her hips against me.

My girl is needy right now, and I fully intend on taking care of her.

I sit her on the edge of the bed and bend to pull her shirt over her head. Her hands circle her back to unhook her bra before tossing it onto the floor.

I'm shedding my clothes quickly, not wanting to wait another second to feel her against me.

She sucks in a breath when she sees my dick bob in attention, reaching her hand out toward me. I pull back for a minute, stopping her when she does.

As soon as she gets her hands on me, I don't know if I'll be able to keep it together for long, and I want to say this before she thinks it's in the heat of the moment.

Hurt crosses her face when I stop her.

"Hey baby, no," I reassure her, kissing away the pain marking her face. I tilt her head up to look at me, brushing my thumb over her cheek and across her lip.

"God, you're so fucking beautiful."

She runs her hands over my forearms, sliding them around my wrists. When I kiss her again, she nips at my lip, teasing me for keeping her waiting.

"I love you, Emmy," I whisper against her mouth. "I love you so fuckin' much. You're the best thing that's ever happened to me, and I—" I pause, emotions hitting me square in the chest. "I just need you to know that, okay?"

"I love you too, Jaxsen."

I kiss her hard; the need pumping through me nearly suffocates me. It feels like I've been waiting so long to say those three words to her. I want to hear her say them again and again.

"Show me," I murmur. I reach for the button on her denim shorts, and she falls back and giggles.

I slide her pants down her legs and toss them to the side. She parts her legs for me, and I curse under my breath at the sight of her swollen bud.

Emmy is absolute perfection. Every single fuckin' inch of her.

I want to spend forever running my hands and lips over every inch of her curves.

She attempts to close her legs, her cheeks flushed from my heated stare.

"Open for me, baby."

She sits up on her elbows, staring down her body at me. She bites her lip again, something I've learned she does when she's teasing me or nervous.

"I love all of you. There isn't a single inch of your body I want you to hide from me. I want it all with you."

She reaches between her legs, grips my chin, and says, "Will you promise me something?"

I nod. "Anything."

"You haven't even heard what it is yet." She laughs.

"Anything for you."

She smirks and shakes her head. "Promise me that no matter what comes our way or what we go through, we won't lose this. Promise me we'll never give up on each other."

She drags her hand over my cheek, and I nod. I turn my head to kiss her palm before I answer her.

"I promise."

She falls back on the bed and opens her legs for me. I brush my finger through her folds, opening her pussy, earning a slow lap of my tongue over her clit.

Her back arches off the bed and her legs tremble, pressing her thighs against the side of my face.

I lean back to rub my finger over her clit and down to her entrance, dipping my finger inside, letting her wetness coat my skin. My wrist turns and my finger curls as she flings her arm over her mouth to stifle her moan.

"Let me hear you, Emmy."

She raises her hips, inviting me to taste her again. I latch my lips onto her clit and suck, and she rewards me with a loud groan.

I continue to tease her, alternating between slowly rubbing her clit with my finger before sucking her into my mouth.

"I need you," she begs. "Please, I need more. I need to feel you."

I stand, fisting my dick in my hand.

She watches me with hooded eyes, slowly trailing her tongue over her lower lip when I rub my thumb through the bead of precum pooling at the tip.

She crawls up the center of the bed and I follow behind her, turning her onto her side. I move her leg over my shoulder, holding her open as I slide into her tight pussy.

"Fuuucckkk," I moan, tossing my head back.

I rotate my hips, helping her get acclimated to my size. She drags her hand over my chest, raking her nails over my skin. The sting burns so good.

When I pull back and thrust in deep, it sends the headboard banging against the wall with the force of my movement.

"More, Jaxsen. I need more."

It's all the permission I need, picking up the pace, thrusting harder and harder into her. She moves her other leg over my shoulder, and I bend her in half, pressing both her knees against her chest.

I grip her thighs, loving how her breasts bounce with each thrust. She grabs them both in her hand, tweaking her nipples.

"Ahh, I'm close," she moans, squeezing her eyes shut. "I'm so close, Jaxsen."

"Squeeze your pussy around me."

She clenches harder, gripping my dick so tight I can't hold it anymore. I lose all control, thrusting into her until her body starts to tremble, her hands grasp the bedsheets, and all the oxygen inside her forces out a heavy groan.

I follow behind her, my hips pistoning until I finish inside her. I collapse on top of her before rolling to the side and pulling her body against mine.

We lie like that until our breathing evens out. She turns over in my arms to look at me and holds my face in her hands.

There's something on her mind. I was hoping we could wait a little longer, but I'm sure it's eating away at her as much as it is me.

"I know you asked me not to read the articles, but I knew whatever it was couldn't be good."

I wince, imagining what she may have felt and the thoughts that crossed her mind when she did. She leans in and kisses me softly.

"Those pictures are of you and her, aren't they?"

"They're old. Probably close to two years old now."

Her brows shoot up. "I didn't realize you were seeing each other for that long."

"It's not what you think. It was never serious. She'd accompany me to events from time to time, and we'd hookup on occasion, but that's all it ever was. We were never exclusive, and it never progressed to anything serious."

"It's no wonder why she acted the way she did at the gala."

I pull back, my eyes narrowing. "What's that supposed to mean?"

"She's in love with you, Jaxsen. She's hurting."

"Well, she has an odd way of showing it." I laugh.

"She's trying to make you jealous. She's sees you've moved on and giving me what she wanted with you. She's just trying to hurt you because she's hurting herself."

"She didn't love me, Emmy. She loved what she could get from me, just like everyone else. My name, my money, and everything that comes along with being associated to Jaxsen Wild, the basketball player."

She nods and I squeeze my eyes shut, hating how this conversation is getting under my skin. I release a slow breath, and she runs her hand over my chest, calming me.

"You know none of it matters to me, right? I don't care that you're a basketball player, about the flashy events, or all the media gossip. I will accept it because I support you and your dreams, but I'm not in love with Jaxsen Wild, the ball player. I'm in love with Jaxsen Wild, the kind, protective, and handsome man I'm with right now."

I tilt her chin up to look at me and kiss her again.

It's soft and slow, full of love and understanding.

Our lips break apart and she presses her forehead to mine. "You know that, don't you?"

"I do."

She relaxes, turning back over and takes my hands in hers to wrap them around her waist, holding onto her.

I trail kisses along the curve of her neck to her shoulder. She moves the sheet over us, and we settle into the bed.

When I hear her breathing even out and her soft snores take over, it's then, and only then, I let the fear of losing her creep back in.

I don't ever want to let this go.

CHAPTER TWENTY

EMMY

The day after Jaxsen told me he loved me was the day of my first doctor's appointment. I decided it would be best for me to get a blood test to confirm I'm pregnant, giving me a little time before I figure out how to find the words to tell Jaxsen.

I broke down this morning, though, desperately needing someone to talk to, and finally shared the news with Kaylee. She already started to suspect something was going on after the basketball game. My emotions have been all over the place with the gossip swirling around Jaxsen and now, our relationship.

It's been a difficult couple weeks, making it hard to focus on anything else. This isn't how I dreamed of finding out I am pregnant or the circumstances I wanted us to be in when I told Jaxsen either.

I feel even worse knowing Jaxsen is dealing with so much more. He has Game Five tonight, and I'm trying to keep things light and easy between us, not wanting to add more to his already full plate.

I'll tell him everything he needs to know when the season is over.

For now, I'm so thankful to have Kaylee to lean on, reassuring me everything will be okay. She'll be here with me to figure out what to do next.

"Knock, knock, knock. The party is here." Cody struts through the door, pretending he's on the catwalk. He has a bottle of wine in one hand with a brown paper bag in the other.

I grin. He jumps up and down, holding his arm out wide for me, wrapping it around my neck in a hug.

"I've missed you, bestie. I feel like it's been years since we've hung out."

Kaylee comes barreling through the door and kicks off her heels.

"Hi Cody," she bellows over her shoulder. Her arms are full of bags from the store. She makes a dash toward the dining room. "Sorry, I didn't want to make more than one trip."

She drops everything on the floor, bending at her knees. There are probably close to fifteen bags scattered around her feet. We all start to laugh because that's so something we'd do.

We both follow Cody into the kitchen. Kaylee looks up at me beneath her long, false lashes. I can see the questions swirling in her mind before she glances over to Cody and back to me. She doesn't want to say the words out loud because she's not sure if I've told Cody or not, but internally she's screaming for me to tell her how the doctor's visit went.

Meanwhile, I'm trying to figure out how I'll break it to Cody I won't be having any wine, when I blurt out, "I'm pregnant."

Cody nearly drops his glass on the counter when his eyes bug out, his mouth falling open in shock.

"I'm sorry, what did you just say?"

I grit my teeth together in a forced smile. "I'm pregnant."

I reach behind my back, pulling out the photos the ultrasound tech gave me that I hid behind me, and hold them up.

"I went to the doctor today and they did a blood test. They also had to do an ultrasound to confirm how far along I am. I'm twelve weeks today. Looks like we'll have a December baby here in a few months."

"Ho-ly shiiiiit," Cody exclaims, smacking his hand over his mouth.

Kaylee already has tears forming in her eyes. She steps over the mountain of bags and wraps her arms around me in a tight hug.

"How are you? Are you okay?"

I nod. "I am now."

"Good." She sighs.

She pulls back and takes the pictures from my hand. Any hope of containing the tears is out the window as she looks at the tiny little human growing inside me with tears flowing freely down her cheeks.

"I don't even know what I'm looking at," she jokes.

Cody is still standing wide-eyed, shaking his head in amazement. I think this is the most speechless I've ever seen him. He sets the bottle of wine on the counter and pulls me in for a hug.

"When I told you to live it up, I didn't mean go off and get knocked up," he whispers in my ear.

I chuckle. "We hadn't quite planned on this happening."

"You gave him the wrong number," he jokes. "Of course, you didn't plan for this to happen."

We all start laughing. It's crazy how much has happened in the span of only twelve weeks. If I hadn't got the internship and he didn't come in to get his suit, we may never have run into each other again.

"What did Jaxsen say when you told him?" Cody asks. He puts back one of the wine glasses, realizing we won't be needing it now.

I bite my lip, glancing over at Kaylee. She shrugs.

"I haven't told him yet. I guess I'm not sure how he'll take it. We've also seen how the media is like vultures ..." I trail off.

"You're going to tell him, though, right?"

"Yeah, I'm planning on waiting until after the season is over. He has enough stressing him out as it is, and I don't want to add to it or take his focus off the game."

"That's understandable." Cody nods, filling up the two glasses. "It's only a few more days, right?"

He hands Kaylee hers, and she hands over the ultrasound pictures.

"I still don't know what I'm looking at." Kaylee laughs.

They listen intently when I tell them all about my appointment, including all the nitty-gritty details of the ultrasound. Cody acts grossed out, but I've had to bear through his sordid stories of his flings, so he can deal with it.

It's what friends do.

Miami wins their game 98-94. Jaxsen is amped up when he calls me after. He wanted me to meet him at his place when he landed, and I'll be honest, I wanted to be with him. It's been a long day, though, and I have a long shift ahead of me tomorrow.

I have a lot on my mind. I'm still trying to work through the news, while holding back and not telling him everything. I'm not one to keep secrets, and I'm afraid I'll blurt it out.

I keep replaying his comment from our conversation about Kelly.

She didn't love me, Emmy. She loved what she could get from me, just like everyone else. My name, my money, and everything that comes along with being associated to Jaxsen Wild, the basketball player.

My heart aches at the thought of him thinking the same about me.

What if he thinks I got pregnant intentionally to trap him?

My stomach is in knots, and I toss and turn for most of the night. The next morning, I'm thankful I don't have to be to the airport until eleven for my shift. It gives me time to sleep in and enjoy a long bath before getting ready.

I can already tell I'm going to need a new uniform before too long. The ones I have are already starting to become tight and uncomfortable.

We're on the last leg of our trip, flying in from New York to Miami, and I couldn't be more thankful.

I know at some point I'm going to have to sort out plans for my job. Once I'm further along in my pregnancy, I won't be able to fly.

I love what I've been doing at Michael Jacobs. I've talked to Jillian a few times about hiring me as an assistant once my internship is up. Although it wouldn't give me the experience I want, it would allow me to stay on with them while I finish school. Hopefully, then when the time comes, I'd be able to apply for a new position.

We go through the preflight motions, welcoming the passengers on board and serving them refreshments. Cody and I cover first class tonight, reminding me of the day I met Jaxsen.

When Carter begins playing "Lucy in the Sky with Diamonds," I settle into my seat, and a short while later we are taxiing down the runway.

"My sister will be in town this weekend," I say to Cody, resting my head on the headrest. I want to close my eyes and relax, but I know the moment I do, sleep will pull me under.

"She will?" Cody exclaims. He's met my sister already. They worked together before I ever got my job for the airline. "Have you told her about the little bun?"

Cody has started referring to the baby as "little bun" since he found out the news. He's been super supportive too. He surprised me with a care package full of bath products and a face mask, hoping to help me get comfortable and relax.

I don't know what I'd do without my friends right now.

"She called a couple days ago to tell me she'd be visiting, and I told her everything. To say she was shocked would be an understatement."

Alexa was always the protective big sister, looking out for me, almost too much in a way. I know she cares and wants to keep me from getting hurt, but I've reminded her one too many times I'm capable of taking care of myself. If I fall on my face, I'll pick myself back up again.

All I want from her is to be supportive and listen when I need an ear or a shoulder to lean on. We've had the talk before where I've reminded her I won't go through life learning from her mistakes. Even if she's right and I get hurt, I'd rather it be my decision.

No risks come with no rewards. Sometimes you have to take the risks if you want to find love.

"She's gonna stop by when I get home, although I'm not sure if it will be tonight or tomorrow. I wouldn't mind having the evening to myself. Jaxsen won't be flying in until late."

I hear the familiar sound of a camera clicking after I say Jaxsen's name. Both of our heads snap toward the group of passengers seated in the front, one of them is a man holding a camera, pointed right at me.

"Emmy Kincaid, right?" the man says.

He's older, with dark hair peppered with silver, with deep scars on his cheeks leading up to his temple. He's dressed in all black with a pair of sunglasses hanging from the collar of his shirt.

My stomach rolls, feeling like the walls are closing in on me.

"Who are you?" Cody interjects, immediately concerned by his question and the tone of his voice.

"I'm not talking to you. I'm asking the lady. Are you Emmy Kincaid?"

"Who are you, and what do you want?" I ask, my voice louder than I intended for it to be.

The seatbelt lights are still on, meaning we need to remain seated as the plane carries us into the air.

"What do you have to say about your relationship with Jaxsen? Did you know he had a girlfriend when the two of you started seeing each other?"

"Excuse me?" I narrow my eyes at him.

Cody rests his hand on my thigh. The man zeros in on it, pointing his camera at the two of us, snapping away.

"Sir, I'm going to have to ask you to put the camera away immediately," Cody commands.

He's not normally someone to get angry. In fact, I can't recall the last time I heard him use this tone with anyone. It makes the blood in my veins turn to ice.

"I don't have to put my camera away. This is my property and I'm allowed to have it wherever I'd like. Are you going to take away everyone else's cameras and camera phones, or just mine?"

"Will you listen to the man and leave them alone?" a passenger next to him bellows. "Who are you, and why are you harassing them?"

"My name is Robert, and I'm a photographer with Hollywood Tea." He reaches into his pocket and holds up a badge.

I slap my hand over my mouth, nausea rolling through me.

"Oh, shit," I mumble under my breath. "I feel like I'm gonna be sick."

"Fuck," Cody mutters.

Robert turns his attention back on me, continuing with his persistent questioning.

"Is it true he cheated on Kelly with you, and you're the reason behind their relationship falling apart?"

"What?" I shout. "You can't possibly be serious."

He smiles, holding up the camera to snap another series of photos.

I always said I wouldn't wither away from any sign of trouble that could come our way, but I never expected it would come to this.

I feel trapped, with nowhere to go, and we're nearly thirty-thousand feet in the air.

The bell dings and Carter's voice comes over the speaker, announcing to passengers they are free to move about the cabin.

"Stay here," Cody commands. He stands, pulling the curtain back, separating me from the rest of the plane.

I move over to his seat and take a stack of crackers from the cart and begin to slowly eat a few. I talked to my doctor about my nausea. He warned me this is something that comes along with pregnancy. When I told him about my go-to savior being water and crackers, he encouraged me to keep them handy when it comes up again, but also assured me it would likely get better as I moved into the second trimester.

Lord, I can only hope so.

I pour a small amount of water in my hand and rub my hands together, patting it over my face to help cool me down.

My stomach twists in knots, replaying the man's comments, insinuating I would start a relationship with Jaxsen while he's still with someone else.

Do they really believe I'm the other woman? Anyone who knows me knows I would never intentionally come between two people and break them apart.

Is there more to their relationship than I know?

After how things ended with Matthew, I was so devastated and heartbroken. I spent nearly two weeks crying in a ball on my bed, unable to keep anything down.

I was an absolute mess.

I'd never do this to someone else. It's not who I am.

What if I'm wrong about Jaxsen like I was with Matthew?

What if everything I know about him and our relationship is a complete lie?

CHAPTER TWENTY-ONE

JAXSEN

"Sir, I have her," Greg says.

Those four words have me sighing in relief.

Emmy was not even off the plane when the pictures of her surfaced, showing her trapped, being interrogated on her flight home. I fired off a text to Greg and asked him to pick her up from the airport.

I didn't want her to be left alone to deal with those vultures.

This is exactly why I keep my relationships private and out of the public eye. They can't help but dig their nose into my business. They've taken something as pure and wonderful as my love for Emmy, and they're threatening to ruin it with more lies.

"Am I on speaker phone?" I ask.

"Yes, sir."

"Emmy," I sigh, my voice softening for her. "Are you okay?"

"I am," she says. "Well, I will be when you get home."

I rub my fingers over my forehead, attempting to massage the pounding I feel rattling in my skull. I won't land back in Miami until later tonight, but the distance between us is killing me.

The tension and stress going on with the championship on the line, while dealing with the drama, has my anxiety through the roof.

It's one thing when they come after me. I'm used to their lies and manipulation swirling around, all for the sake of clicks. They've made money off smearing my name for years.

It's different, though, when they come after someone you love. I can't sit by idly and continue to let them do it, not anymore.

"I'll have Greg take you back to my place and you can stay there until I get home. I have security. You'll be safe there in case anyone tries to approach you again."

"I want to stay at my place."

Alarm bells go off in my head. She sounds different, distant, guarded.

"Okay," I say.

She must pick up on the hesitation in my voice. "My sister is in town, and she wants to come over and see me. It's just easier that way. Plus, I want to sleep in my own bed. It's been a long couple of days."

"I'll swing by my place when I land to grab a change of clothes, and I'll be over."

"All right, that sounds good." I can hear the smile in her voice now.

She knows better than to think I'm gonna sleep away from her for another night.

I hate being away from her. The bed is cold, and I toss and turn without her body pressed against mine. I know I can't have her with me every night; it's bound to happen where we'll be apart with our careers and schedules putting us all over the country.

I refuse to be away from her when we're in the same city, though.

We don't land in Miami until after nine. By the time Greg picks me up and takes me back to my place, it's pushing ten o'clock. I'm in too much of a hurry to get to Emmy's, I don't see Kelly standing near the door until I get a glimpse of her long blonde hair out of the corner of my eye.

"What the hell are you doing here?" I grunt.

I quickly glance around, expecting to find a line of paparazzi with her ready to ambush me.

"You haven't been answering my calls or texts, so I came to try and talk to you."

"Maybe you should take the hint." I spit out. "I have your number blocked, but even if I didn't, I wouldn't have responded to you in the first place."

"Why are you such an asshole now?"

I shake my head and chuckle. *Is this real life?*

"I'm sorry; have you been living under a rock, or are you really that clueless?"

She's dressed in a pink dress and her long hair is curled down her back. She looks like she's ready to go out somewhere, not at all in a way I'd expect to see her when she shows up unannounced at my place.

It makes me wonder if she isn't trying to put me in another compromising position to smear more of her lies. She shouldn't even be able to get in here. Immediately my defenses are up, wondering how she managed to get past security.

"Jaxsen, please." She begs. The sound of her voice grates on my nerves and I cringe.

"You wanted to talk to me. You came and broke in here to talk to me. So, talk. What do you want from me? The sooner we get this over, the sooner you can get out of my life and leave me alone."

Her shoulders sag. She has the nerve to almost look defeated.

"I saw what was in the news. They're saying she's your girlfriend. Is that true?"

I run my hand over my face. Are we seriously doing this right now?

"How about we start with the fact you leaked nudes of me to the media? How about we start there before we get into what they are saying about my relationship?"

"It's true, isn't it? You're in a relationship with her."

She moves to block me from getting into my car, leaning against the door, and crosses her arms.

"Kelly, will you listen to yourself? Answer the fuckin' question. I want you to admit it to me. You'd think after all this shit you're causing me and for you to show up here like this, you could admit it was you."

She reaches her hand up, brushing away a fake tear from her eye. I don't think I ever saw her upset or cry when we were together, so any emotion she's putting on for me right now is all a show.

I'm willing to bet money she's up to something, but I can't be sure. Either way, I need to get her out of here.

I lift my phone and fire off a text to Greg with two words.

Me: *Kelly's here.*

Greg's going to be livid he left me alone. He insisted on going up with me to my place, but I instructed him to head home, and I'd be fine. I was heading over to Emmy's anyway.

I haven't seen her in what feels like forever, and Kelly is blocking me from leaving to be with her.

I have the forethought in mind to open the video app on my phone and press play before slipping it back into the pocket of my shorts.

"I need you to go or I'll have security down here to escort you off the property."

"Jaxsen, please, will you give me a chance to explain. I didn't think it would come to this. It wasn't supposed to get leaked the way it did."

"Explain what? What did you expect to happen, Kelly? I already suspected Crew was involved. He can't win a championship on his own merit. He has to stir shit up and make it impossible for me to focus on the game. It was the two of you, wasn't it? You both did this on purpose."

"It's not what you think, Jaxsen, I swear. Please, let's just go up to your place and talk about this."

"I'm not going anywhere with you."

She starts to look around. I can't tell if she's humiliated by my blatant rejection or if she expects Crew to show up any moment.

"The fact I'm even entertaining this conversation when I know it was you from the beginning is pushing it for me. I don't want to see you and I don't want to speak with you. Do me a favor, will you? Leave me alone and keep my name and Emerson's name out of your mouth."

The sound of tires screeching in the distance sends her whipping around. I spot Greg's black SUV coming around the corner, with a white car following behind him. He must've alerted security when he came rushing through the entrance.

Kelly's eyes are wild, a mixture of shock and panic sweeps over her face.

"Ms. Eaton, I need to ask you to leave the premises immediately. You are forbidden from the property," Greg orders as he steps out.

She turns her face back toward me as if she expects me to fight him on it or tell her he's wrong.

Security comes up behind Greg, dressed in a black uniform. I recognize the man, Maxwell, but I've only spoken to him a couple times. Most of the time he speaks with Greg directly.

"Ma'am, I need you to come with me," Maxwell says, coming up to stand behind her, ushering her away from me.

"Wait," I say, stopping her.

Greg's head snaps over to me, his jaw clenched in agitation. He's only trying to protect me, and I know he's fighting off the urge to drag me away.

He trusts me, though, and I don't doubt in the back of his mind he's telling himself whatever is driving me right now is with purpose.

"I don't want to make this situation worse than it already is, Kelly. We can resolve this in one of two ways. You can leave me alone and never utter my name or Emerson's name again. That includes making sure any other pictures or videos you may have of me never see the light of day. Or we can go about it the legal way. Just know, if it comes to that, I'll spend every penny I have to send a message. To you and to Crew, not to fuck with me ever again."

For the first time knowing Kelly, the hurt on her face looks genuine. Whatever choice she makes from here will be up to her, but I know she's aware I'm not messing around.

I won't let her ruin my career or my livelihood, and I most certainly won't let her take my relationship down in the process.

I hope it doesn't have to resort to the legal route. I would hate to put Emmy through it, but I can only hope she'd continue to stand by me no matter what comes our way.

Greg reaches for my arm and pushes me to step back, standing between me and Kelly. He turns, keeping his back toward me, and nods his head to Maxwell.

Kelly whips her arm out of his grip and takes off toward her car. I didn't see it until now, parked in the corner of the lot, away from the security cameras.

Her heels click on the cement as she hits the button on her keypad and scurries into her car, peeling out as she takes off out of the parking garage.

"I need to go be with Emmy. I was supposed to be there almost thirty minutes ago now."

Greg nods. "I'll see to this and get to the bottom of it, sir. I'll let you know what I find."

I reach into my pocket and check my phone, finding the video still recording. I hit end, making sure it saved fully. I flash my screen at Greg and nod.

"It'll all be okay, though. I have the entire conversation recorded. Even if she comes after me again, I have her on video admitting it was her."

It doesn't happen often, but a wide grin stretches across Greg's face. He pats me on the shoulder, a look of pride beaming on his face. We both know this whole ordeal took a couple years off my life.

"Ms. Kincaid awaits you."

I flash him a wink and climb into my car.

Now, I need to make sure my girl is okay.

CHAPTER TWENTY-TWO

JAXSEN

The shades are drawn, but the light is still on when I put the car in park.

I jog up the stairs to her place and knock on the door, glancing around to see if anyone is nearby or sees me when the door opens, and a woman is standing there.

Her hand is on her hip, her eyes narrowing, and for a second, I wonder if I'm at the right door.

I glance over at the number, confirming I'm in fact at the right place, when I see Emmy appear behind her.

"Alexa, knock it off. Let him inside."

"I didn't say anything." She narrows her eyes at me, standing back, holding her hand out to usher me inside.

Emmy shakes her head and smiles. Her hair is pulled up in a towel, with a red silk robe wrapped around her, cinched at the waist. There's a hint of her chest showing, and my gaze lingers a little too long on her body, earning me a smirk when my eyes finally meet hers.

"Hi, baby," I murmur, dropping my bag by the door.

I kick off my sneakers and adjust the hat on my head, moving the bill around backward to give me better access to her when I lean in for a kiss.

She grins at me, and I hear who I now know is her sister sigh behind us, clearly not amused with my affection.

It's too damn bad, I haven't seen my girl in almost two days, and I won't wait a second longer to hug and kiss her.

I wrap my arms around Emmy's waist, pulling her into my body and tilt her chin up to kiss me. She wraps her hand around my wrist, holding on tight as she sucks in a breath when our lips meet.

"I missed you," I whisper, when I pull back, pressing my forehead against hers.

"Missed you more."

"Well, isn't that sweet. Are you going to introduce us or are you going to get it on right here in the living room?" Alexa quips, and I smile down at Emmy.

"Not how I expected to meet your sister, but I'm always game if you are."

She swats my chest. "It's my sister."

I shrug, turning back to Alexa, holding my hand out to shake hers.

"Hi Alexa, forgive me for my lack of manners. I'm Jaxsen; it's nice to meet you."

Her gaze bounces from me, over to Emmy, and back again. She finally gives in and shakes mine.

"So, you're the Jaxsen Wild I've been hearing so much about."

I wince, knowing if she's been paying attention to what the reports have been saying, it's no wonder her first impression of me is less than impressed.

"I know what you may have heard about me has you concerned, but I can assure you, most of it is untrue. I'd never do anything to intentionally hurt Emmy, including lie to her or see someone else behind her back."

Alexa glances over at Emmy before she nods.

"I'm gonna go meet up with some friends while I'm in town." She walks over and wraps her arms around Emmy in a hug. "I'll be back to see you tomorrow before I leave, okay?"

"I'll call you," Emmy reassures her.

"If you need anything at all, you better." She steps back, pointing her finger at Emmy and then back over to me. "And you … you better take care of my sister, or I'll be on the first flight back to Miami. If you think you've been through hell with these reporters, you have no idea what you're in for."

"All right, all right. Bye, Alexa, I'll call you tomorrow," Emmy says, ushering her out the door. When the door closes, she sags against it.

"Are you okay?" I ask, her cheeks are rosy, and her face looks pale.

"Yeah, I'm fine. I'm just feeling warm from my shower is all." She reaches up, untwisting the towel in her hair and runs her fingers through the dark wet strands. "I think I need to sit down, though."

She takes two steps toward me, before her knees go weak, and she collapses. I rush toward her as she stumbles, nearly falling when my arms wrap around her waist to catch her.

"Emmy, Emmy, are you okay?" I ask, frantic.

I lower her to the ground and reach into my pocket when I see Greg's name flash on the screen.

"Where are you? Can you call 911 for me? Emmy fainted, and I need someone to get to her house, now. I don't know what's happening."

"It's okay," she mumbles, her words slow and garbled. "I'm okay. Get water and crackers."

"Crackers, fuckin' crackers? What the hell are crackers going to do?" I ask, lifting her in my arms and setting her on the sofa.

Perspiration dots her forehead, and she loosens the sash, slipping her arms out of her robe, revealing the lace bra underneath. The silk material gathers around her waist.

If I wasn't so freaked out by what just happened, I'd be distracted by the sight of her and her breasts nearly spilling out of the top.

"Don't move, okay? Stay right there." I hold my hands up, with Greg in the background asking more details. He must have the dispatch on another phone when I hear him rattle off Emmy's address.

There's a box of crackers sitting on the counter. I grab a bottle of water from the refrigerator before racing back into the living room. Emmy is slouched against the back of the couch, her legs and arms spread open as if she's about to do a snow angel.

"Here, eat these." I shove her a stack of crackers, almost dropping the entire package on the floor in the process.

"Calm down, Jaxsen. I'm okay, I promise. I'm just having another dizzy spell."

"Another?" I question. "Has this happened again since the time I picked you up?"

She nods, slowly lifting the cracker to her mouth, and takes a swig of water.

"Nausea." She says around the food before swallowing it down. "I've been nauseous, and I haven't been able to keep anything but crackers down."

I fall to my knees in front of her, running my hand over her thigh. Fear and worry prick through me as Greg gets back on the line.

"They should be there in a few minutes, Jaxsen. They're on their way."

"Okay, thanks," I respond without thinking, still staring at Emmy.

She doesn't realize or pick up on the panic on my face, slowly chewing her crackers in between taking drinks of water. She fans her face, sweat still dripping from her forehead down the side of her cheek.

She unties the sash at her waist and attempts to move the robe, revealing the rest of her body to me, down to her matching lace underwear. I feel like an asshole for thinking about how beautiful she looks when my eyes fall on the round bump forming at her stomach.

When I glance back up at Emmy, her eyes are on mine, and I'm unable to form the words on the tip of my tongue, begging to be spoken.

She must see the question burning in my gaze, her face falling before her hand protectively drops to her stomach. Almost as if she's scared of what I might say next.

"Emmy ..."

"Jaxsen, I–" she squeezes her eyes shut, tears trickling down her face mixing in with the sweat dripping from her brow. "I was going to tell you, I promise."

"Tell me what."

She looks at the phone still in my hand, my other gripping her knee as I stare up at her, with crackers strewn across her lap.

"I'm pregnant."

The words pass her mouth, just as loud knocks hit the door, and two people enter. They're dressed in a navy collared shirt and pants, wearing a badge with EMT printed in large letters, carrying a duffle bag in their hands.

"Are you Emerson Kincaid?" the woman asks.

Emmy nods. I take a step back, giving them room. Thoughts and questions swirl through my mind, but Emmy doesn't take her eyes off me. The tears still flow freely down her face, and I want so badly to hold her, to be there with her, but I can't.

I don't know what to say; I don't know what to do.

"Sir, may I ask for your name?"

"Jaxsen," I mutter. "Jaxsen Wild."

The man's brows furrow as he does a double-take, looking back at me. My hat is still on, and I'm dressed down in a pair of gym shorts and a T-shirt.

"As in *the* Jaxsen Wild?"

"I guess, yeah. That's me."

I pause, not wanting to do this right now. "Please take care of her. Please make sure she's okay. She's the love of my life."

He nods, holding his hand up to reassure me. "We'll make sure she's okay, man."

My gaze meets Emmy's again.

"She's the love of my life, and she's pregnant with my baby."

It took some pushing, but I was able to convince Emmy to go to the hospital to get checked out. It turns out she was slightly dehydrated, which they said is likely from the fact she's been unable to keep anything down for the past few days.

I think back to the day I picked her up from the airport. Cody was concerned about her, making sure to see that I looked after her. She didn't tell me she hadn't been feeling well, so when I sat in the hospital chair next to her bed, listening to her share with the doctor how she's been feeling, the guilt poured through me like hot lava.

I've been so focused on the game and the shit going on in the news, I was completely oblivious to what was going on with her.

She's been there for me through everything, and I feel like I let her down, like I failed her. It was beginning to eat me alive.

They did an ultrasound while we were there, to check and make sure the baby was okay. They were concerned about her elevated blood pressure, but we were able to get it under control once they gave her some IV fluids. In the end, they reassured us everything was fine, and I was relieved. Both that they were okay, and thankful I got the chance to see the life growing inside her with my very eyes.

They said she's going on thirteen weeks.

Thirteen weeks ago, puts it back to the day we met in the airport.

I knew better than to believe there was a chance it could be anyone else's. She had broken up with her ex a month before and hadn't been with anyone else since.

She was pregnant with my baby.

Ready or not, I was going to be a father.

CHAPTER TWENTY-THREE

EMMY

The mattress next to me moves just before I feel the light touch of Jaxsen's lips press against my cheek. He trails a line of kisses down my jaw until he meets my lips.

"Wake up, baby."

I groan. "I don't wanna," I mumble, a smile breaking across my face.

After we left the hospital last night, he drove me back to his place. It was early in the morning by the time we got home. I didn't want to do anything but crawl into bed.

He has been so patient and attentive since finding out the news. All night he didn't leave my bedside, except for the few minutes when he stepped out to call Alexa for me. Even when we went to bed, he was there. His body molding to the back of mine, his hand resting protectively over my stomach.

"Well, you gotta wake up if you want to eat the breakfast I made you."

I slowly blink my eyes open and smile up at him. He's wearing a black T-shirt and the same hat he wore the night before. The sight of him with the dimple on his cheek when he smiles makes my stomach flutter.

"Or you could crawl back into bed with me." I grin, wagging my brows.

"I was reading how pregnant women start to get hornier in the second trimester. Is this what I have to look forward to?" He winks. "If so, I think we should start talking about you moving in with me now."

I playfully smack him on the arm, and he moves back, sitting on the mattress next to me.

"You were reading about pregnancy?"

He reaches for my hand, folding it in his, staring down as he traces his finger over my skin. "I couldn't sleep this morning. The game today, the news last night, you in the hospital. It's all been swirling through my mind."

I wince. This is exactly what I was afraid of, him being so in his head that he wouldn't be able to focus on the game.

"Why didn't you tell me sooner? Why didn't you tell me you weren't feeling well or about the baby?"

"You just said, Jaxsen, how you were unable to sleep last night. You have the biggest game of your career today, the chance to win an NBA championship, and I knew the weight this news would have on you. On our relationship."

His brows furrow. "Our relationship? What do you mean?"

I release a slow breath. I guess now is the time I tell him, even though I was hoping to wait. "I kept thinking back to how you told me you've felt used by the women you've been with before. The last thing I wanted was for you to believe I did this intentionally, that I did it to trap you, to feel obligated to be with me."

He flinches. The silence between us is deafening.

"I love you, Emerson."

Tears prick my eyes, my heart seizing at his proclamation. He lifts my hand to his mouth, kissing the back.

"I love you too." I choke, unable to get the words out without the emotion hitting me.

I swear, these hormones are getting the best of me these days. One second, I'm laughing and smiling, then the next, I'll see something that has me crying without warning.

"I'm starting to think I didn't know what love was until I met you," I murmur. "My relationships before, they pale in comparison to what I feel for you. It goes to show, it doesn't matter how long you've been with someone; when love comes into your life, it happens quickly and without warning. I wasn't looking when I found you, Jaxsen. I wasn't ready to open my heart up again, but you continue to prove to me why hooking up with you in that hotel was the best decision of my life."

He starts laughing at my choice of words and leans in, pressing his forehead to mine. "It was the best night of my life. It brought me you, and it gave me our child."

We both know the truth behind why he was visiting New York that night, the meeting he had that day with the commissioner. For him to still be able to say it was the best day of his life makes my heart soar.

"Only you, Emmy, could tame the wild child." He chuckles.

He pulls me up until I'm sitting, wrapping his arms around me. I move to climb on his lap, wrapping my legs around his waist and my arms around his neck.

"Are you sure you don't want to crawl back into bed with me?" I mumble against his neck.

He runs his hand over my back, moving lower to grab my ass. I grind against him, pulling back to kiss his lips.

He growls. "Don't tempt me, woman. I have food in the kitchen, hot and waiting for you."

"I'm hot and waiting for you." I smirk.

He shakes his head, lifts me into his arms, and carries me out of the bedroom.

"First, I need you to eat. If you can do that, I'll fuck you on the counter, how about that?"

"Mmm, deal." I press my hands against the side of his face, kissing him softly.

We had the rest of the morning and early afternoon to spend together, talking about our future, before he had to be at the arena for his game.

While I wasn't at all happy at the thought of giving up my job, we both agreed there were too many risks with me working for the airline right now. With me being pregnant and traveling on top of the paparazzi hounding me, especially once the news breaks about the pregnancy and our relationship, there's no telling if I'll ever have privacy again.

My life is changing being in a relationship with Jaxsen, and it's something I'll have to accept if we want to be together.

We decided I'd spend the summer focusing on my internship, and when it's up, I'll work on transferring my credits to a school here in Miami. I've already started talking to Jillian about working for Michael Jacobs this fall, and if it all pans out well, I could be working there while going to school.

As much as I would miss traveling and working with Cody, I know he supports me and my career.

A lot is changing, and it is happening fast, but I also can't help but feel like it is all coming together exactly how it was meant to be.

I'm glad I ended up going to the game with Kaylee and Sydney. The energy in the arena is electric, amplified from all the others I've been to this season.

At first, Jaxsen wasn't enthused when I told him I was still planning to go to the game. It took some cajoling to convince him, but when I reminded him the girls would be with me, and how Kaylee would be quick to get me out of there if she thought for a second something was wrong, he eventually gave in.

I think there was a part of him that worried about the crowd getting reckless and something happening to me, although it gave him some relief knowing he could look over and see me sitting in the stands too.

The game is tied going into the second quarter. We get up and walk around, grabbing something to eat and more water, before making our way back to our seats.

Jaxsen was on fire, too. If I thought the news of my pregnancy was going to distract him, I was wrong. If anything, it's almost as if it lit a fire in him.

We talked this morning about how after the finals were over, things would start slowing down. While he would still want to stay focused on the upcoming season, we'd have some time to spend together without him coming and going as much.

I'm looking forward to enjoying the rest of my summer with him.

The crowd begins to cheer, and the music amps up just before the Miami Blaze jog back onto the court. Jaxsen sprints toward the bench, his eyes focused on me. He waves me over, and I grin, hurrying down the handful of stairs separating us.

"Two more quarters," he whispers, pressing his forehead against mine.

I hold his face in my hands. "You can do it. I know you can. I'm here cheering you on."

He smiles, his lips crash down on mine, and the crowd around us erupts.

I pull back, and he flashes me a wink. The smile on my face is so wide, it's nearly splitting my face in half.

When I turn back, I spot Kaylee and Sydney in the crowd. Kaylee's clapping enthusiastically and Sydney's clutching her hands to her chest, a look of awe on her face.

The rest of the game has me on pins and needles. Jaxsen's playing like he knows exactly what's on the line. Between him, Colson, and Miles, they are dominating the game.

At one point, a player gets in Jaxsen's face, and I know everyone, myself included, is worried about him letting his temper get to him.

He shakes his head, a big smile beaming on his face, and he turns to walk away, not even giving in to their antics. They try like hell to dig in, getting under his skin, but he doesn't give them the satisfaction of feeding into it.

I'm so proud of him for how he's handling it because sometimes I wouldn't blame him if he did start telling them off or giving it right back.

The crowd is on their feet going into the last five minutes of the game. They are neck in neck, trading points back and forth. Every time I think we are pulling ahead, something happens to flip things back around.

"I've never been so anxious in my life," I bounce on my feet, leaning in to shout over the crowd into Kaylee's ear.

"He's playing so well, though. Thirty-six points so far, it's unbelievable. He's made almost half the team's points."

I chew my lip and shake my hands out, attempting to release some of the pent-up energy mounting inside me. I keep thinking, if I'm this nervous, Lord only knows how Jaxsen must feel right now.

I look up at the scoreboard, seeing Jaxsen's name on the screen. Colson has eighteen points, Miles with fourteen. She's right, Jaxsen came out tonight knowing what was on the line, and he hasn't slowed down from the second the game tipped off.

When they announce the last two minutes of the game, I'm ready to sit down and cover my eyes. I don't know what's happening when I watch, and every second that goes by feels like my stomach is twisting in a knot of nerves and anxiety.

Miami has the ball, and Miles passes it in to Jaxsen. He dribbles it between his legs from one side to the next. He points his finger over to a player on one side of the court and blindly passes the ball to Colson, throwing them off their game.

Colson quickly goes up for a shot, and it hits the rim before bouncing through the net, making a three-pointer. He pulls his hand back, pretending to shoot a bow and arrow, hitting the shot right on his mark.

Everything from that point on passes by in a blur. Miami is able to pull ahead by six points, and it seems to reignite the crowd and the team into a frenzy. The frustration is wearing on L.A., which only seems to energize Jaxsen and the Blaze more.

As the final seconds tick by, it is clear who the winner is. When the buzzer sounds, I'm jumping up and down with my arms around Kaylee and Sydney, tears streaming down our faces.

I'll never forget the sight of Jaxsen, when he falls to his knees in the middle of the court in relief, knowing everything he's fought through this season brought him here.

He won.

CHAPTER TWENTY-FOUR

JAXSEN

"Congratulations, man!" Rush claps me on the shoulder.

The news is out.

Emmy is pregnant.

The last week has felt like I'm living a different life. Between winning the championship, being awarded Most Valuable Player, and finding out Emmy is pregnant, I can hardly wrap my mind around all the goodness that life has brought me.

And it all started with Emmy.

I've been thinking back to the day I ran into her in the airport, the smug asshole I was to her, to the night we spent together in the hotel.

She's changed me in ways I didn't see coming, and I wouldn't have accomplished any of it without her by my side. She makes me want to wake up and be a better man than I was the day before.

"Thanks, man!" I pull him in for a hug.

I wouldn't have thought issuing a statement and announcing to the world we are in a relationship and expecting a child, only days after winning the championship, would've gone over the way it has, but I've heard nothing but good things since.

The tide is changing. I know it's only a matter of time before they run another story dragging my name through the mud, but for now, I'm appreciating that during this time in my life, we're hearing all the positive we can get.

"I have to tell you, though, I still can't get my head around it. I'm having a kid. I'm gonna be a dad." I chuckle, widening my eyes and shaking my head.

"Life has its way of bringing you the things you didn't even know you needed or wanted, huh?"

I nod. Ain't that the truth.

I never would've thought we'd be taking this step now, so soon in our relationship, but I couldn't be happier.

Who says when it's the right time to have a kid?

Is it when you make a certain amount of money? Is it when you finish college? Or is it when you reach a certain point in your career?

Sure, it would certainly make life easier to have all those things in a row, but if we keep telling ourselves, "I'll be happy when *this* happens" or "I'll be ready when I get *here*," you fail to take a step back and appreciate the best part of life, and that's in the journey itself.

"How did you feel the day you and Sydney decided to foster Isaac?"

"The circumstances were a little different," he says, taking a seat on the bench, leaning back against the locker door.

I toss my gym bag on the floor between my feet, sitting across from him.

"We both witnessed what his life was like, the circumstances he was living in. When we decided to file the paperwork and start the process to become foster parents, we just knew we wanted to do something. He needed someone to reach their hand out, to help him get out of the situation he was in."

I nod. Colson has told me about a few of the incidents that came up after he met Isaac.

"When we found out he was being placed with us, I think what I felt the most was peace. It was like this sense of relief to know he would be with us, he'd be safe, and we didn't have to worry anymore."

"He's lucky to have you, you know that?"

"Thanks, man. I appreciate it."

I pick up my tennis shoes, the last of my stuff in my locker, and set them in my bag, zipping it up. I rest my elbows on my knees, folding my hands in front of me, lost in thought.

"You know, Emmy and this baby, they're lucky to have you too. You're going to make an amazing dad."

I clap Colson on the back, thanking him. He takes off after our chat, and I finish cleaning out my locker. I hate to think it could be the last time I'll be back here, but I feel my chances of being a part of the Blaze next season are looking good. No matter what happens or where I end up, it will all work out.

I stop by Coach's office on my way out, and he responds the same way Colson did, with a clap on the back and a genuine smile on his face, congratulating me.

I check my phone on my way to my car to see text messages from Emmy and my assistant, Candyce. I asked her for help in planning a surprise dinner tonight to celebrate with Emmy.

I didn't tell Emmy what the plan was, only to dress up because I wanted to take her out to dinner. She's started moving some of her clothes over to my place, and I have to admit, walking into my closet to see her stuff hanging next to mine gives a whole new feeling of happiness.

I never thought I'd get to a place where I'd have someone living in my space with me, making our place a home. I'm starting to see our future together, and it has me looking forward to the life we are building.

"Knock, knock." I smile, leaning my shoulder against the door frame.

She pauses, a makeup brush in her hand, turning to face me as she brushes it over her cheeks before tossing it into the bag sitting open on the counter.

"Hi," she grins.

My eyes trail over her body, the fitted black dress she's wearing hugging all her curves and accentuating the small bump forming in her stomach. It's small, but I grin, recognizing all the ways her body is starting to change. My heart leaps thinking about watching our son or daughter grow inside her.

"You look beautiful," I murmur, closing the distance between us. I lean in to press a kiss against her soft lips.

She moans against my mouth, turning to wrap her arms around my neck, pulling me in to deepen it. I let my hands trail over her lower back, down to grip her ass and grind against her.

"If you keep that up, we won't be making it in time for dinner." She laughs, and I pull back, shaking my head.

She's right. This past week, it's like a switch has been flipped, and neither of us have been able to keep our hands off the other.

Like I said, there's something about having her here and next to me every night that I can't get enough of.

"I have a surprise planned for you. I'm gonna change quick while you finish up. Give me, say, fifteen minutes."

She nods. "I'll be ready by then."

I'm standing in the kitchen, adjusting the cufflinks on my jacket, when I hear her heels clicking on the floor.

My eyes trail over her body, her tan legs down to her red toes with the gold straps wrapped around her feet. I'm starting to get visions of those heels digging into my back when the sound of her throat clearing has me snapping out of my thoughts.

"We have dinner plans, remember?" She smirks.

Why did I think dinner was necessary when I could spend the night devouring her instead?

"Don't tempt me, Em," I warn.

She drags her lip through her teeth, attempting to fight off her smile.

I cross the room toward her, linking our fingers together, and press a soft kiss against the back of her hand.

"Greg's here. Let's go."

She nods, following me outside.

The sun has long since disappeared, and the moonlight is glowing overhead, shining bright on the water crashing along the shoreline. The stars twinkle in the midnight sky.

Greg pulls up at our destination and puts the SUV in park. He opens my door, and I meet Emmy on her side to help her out.

She looks around us, noticing the trail of roses lining the walkway, disappearing into the distance.

"What is this?" She furrows her brows, looking back up at me.

"You'll see," I bend down, kissing her.

We both thank Greg, who gives us one of his signature jovial smiles before nodding his head.

I slip my fingers between Emmy's, and she wraps her hand around my forearm, walking with me down onto the beach, revealing the path lined with candles.

Her hand flies to her mouth when she sees the dozens of roses shaped in a large heart, with a small table centered in the middle, candles circling us.

Tiki torches are scattered around us, providing enough lighting, but aside from that, it's completely private, overlooking the beach.

"Jaxsen," she croaks, and I stare down at her. "This is beautiful."

Tears trail down her cheeks, but she quickly flicks them away.

We've joked about how her hormones are changing, having her laughing or crying in a span of minutes. I can't lie; seeing her reaction and knowing how much she loves it makes it all the more worth it.

"Don't cry," I whisper, brushing the tears away from her eyes.

She pats her skin, waving her hand, attempting to get a wrangle on her emotions. She releases a slow breath and stares back up at me.

"You constantly keep me guessing what you're gonna do next," she laughs.

I wink, dropping down on my knee.

"Oh my God," she says, slapping her hand to her mouth.

I realize what she must think, at that moment, when I reach for the strap of her shoes.

"I'm sorry, baby, I wanted to get your shoes for you."

She swats at me. I look up at her, pulling her against me, holding my hands on the side of her stomach.

"I promise that day is coming soon, though."

She nods. "One thing at a time, though, right?"

"Right," I agree, not wanting to tell her I've started planning how I want to ask her, just not tonight.

I trail my hand down her hips, loving every curve on this woman.

She pulls back, and I finish unhooking the straps of her shoes, helping her step out of one and then the other. I carry them with us, sliding my other hand in hers, and lead her to the table.

"I can't believe you did all this." She looks around us in awe.

I pull out her seat, and I take the one next to her. I reach across the table and slide my fingers between hers.

"I may have had a little help setting it all up, but it was all my idea."

She purses her lips together, fighting off the urge to smile.

"I know our relationship hasn't started off in a conventional way. We've weathered our fair share of challenges, between us both traveling and the media shitstorm that happened."

I wince, hating even bringing up the photos being leaked, but it's the truth.

"I can't promise that there won't be more of it to happen. I haven't been perfect, and sadly, people like to make money off dragging my name through the mud. What I can promise you, though, you and our family, that going forward, I will work to be a better man than the one I was before."

"Jaxsen," she whispers.

"No, baby, let me finish."

She sighs and nods before moving to stand and taking the step separating us. I move my chair back, giving her room, and she climbs on my lap, wrapping her arms around my neck.

"Okay, sorry. Please continue." She smiles.

I run my hands over the soft skin of her thighs, trying to collect my thoughts.

"I promise you and our baby, I will do everything I can to provide for you, to take care of you. I promise to be loyal and faithful to you every day. You won't ever have to question where I stand because I promise I'll always be here beside you."

She holds my face in between her hands, staring into my eyes before kissing me.

When she pulls back, she bites her lip, and I can tell there's something on her mind, but she's holding back saying it.

"What's that look?"

"You know, for being such a bad boy, you do have a sweet side to you."

I run my hand over her stomach. "Only for you, baby. I reserve this only for you. The rest of the world gets the untamed asshole with no filter and I-don't-give-a-damn attitude."

"You may say that, but I think anyone who truly knows you would agree, you're not that man anymore. You're shedding some of that side of you, leaving the asshole Jaxsen behind you."

"Don't go repeating that, will ya? I want my rivals to still think they shouldn't fuck with me."

She smirks and shakes her head.

"I'm lucky to get to see the real Jaxsen Wild, and not the one you put on when you're on the basketball court."

"Always, baby." I kiss her again. "Always for you."

EPILOGUE

JAXSEN
TWO MONTHS LATER

A lot has happened in a span of two months.

After the season wrapped up, we began looking at places to live in Miami. Although my contract with the Blaze is up for renewal soon, I made it very clear this is where I want to be.

This is my home, our home, and I want to put down roots here.

We began looking at places right away, and after only a handful of showings, we found the perfect house. It's along the water, with a beautiful view of the ocean. It gave us the seclusion we wanted from the rest of the world, with plenty of space for us to raise our family for as long as we planned to be here.

It comes with a pool and a jacuzzi, a basketball court, and plenty to keep us busy. I would've bought this house twice over to wake up every morning to Emmy in her swimsuit, her stomach round with the life growing inside her, sitting on the edge of the pool.

She has moved past the morning sickness stage and has begun to feel better and better, but we know the further along she gets, that may change.

For now, we're enjoying everything that comes with preparing for the little boy or girl that will be joining us in four months. We'll know soon, as the doorbell rings, announcing our friends and family who are arriving for our gender reveal party.

I didn't realize these were such a big thing these days, but Emmy insisted we throw a get-together as a house-warming party and to celebrate the gender of our baby.

"Knock, knock," I hear a familiar deep voice filter in, as Rush and Sydney walk through the door, their son Isaac with them. They recently adopted him, welcoming him into their family after they met through a Community Cares event they organized together for the Miami Blaze.

Rush, ever the proud father, claps his son on the shoulder and motions for him to take the gift bag over to the table set on the back patio.

Miles, Darius, and Damien filter in behind him, all wearing proud smiles on their faces.

"I wasn't expecting to see you." I clap Damien on the back. He has been living up north in Minnesota.

"Of course, I wasn't gonna miss this, man. I'm sorry I couldn't be here for the championship, but you know I was cheering you on back home."

I pull him into a hug, and he whispers how happy he is for me.

"MVP, how's it going? Are you ready for your own little ball player to be running around here?" Miles jokes, pulling me in for a hug too.

"Man, I guess we'll have to see. With my luck, I'll have a little girl who will have me falling over myself trying to keep all the boys away from her. If she's anything like her mama, I'm gonna have my work cut out for me."

"Good luck," Darius jokes.

Emmy walks in then, dressed in a pair of white shorts and a white jersey with "Team Boy or Team Girl" printed on the front, matching my own. Her hair pulled up with a few strands of hair falling to frame her face.

Darius greets her with a hug, followed by Miles and Damien. She spots Sydney walking back in with Rush and Isaac before she scurries over to hug her and smile at Isaac.

"You definitely have your work cut out for you," Miles jests, and I smack him on the chest.

"You can look all you want, just as long as you remember that woman is mine."

He holds his hands up. "No disrespect, bro. None at all. I'm happy for you."

I smack him on the chest, and they follow me outside, Rush joining us as we make our way out to the courtyard overlooking the pool.

"How are you taking the news?" Rush asks.

Miles folds his arms, and the guys form a circle around me.

There's been rumors circulating for the last couple of weeks, talks of trades, but the newest one to come out is speculation that Miami will be making a trade with Chicago bringing Crew Savage to play for the Blaze.

"I don't know, man. You know how these things are. There's so much talk going on, you can't really know until it's official. Things can change at the drop of a dime."

After the article came out about me and Emmy, announcing our pregnancy, I heard word from someone that Crew and Kelly split. I always thought she was with him to try and get back at me, to make me jealous.

I couldn't help but think either he found out the truth about why they were together, or she realized it was a lost cause because I didn't give a shit.

Either way, they weren't together anymore, and what they did with their lives was the least of my concerns.

"Do you think your beef is something you guys could put behind you?" Miles asks.

My lip curls, agitation spiking my system at the thought of having to even be around him, much less play with Savage. He's proven one too many times, he gets off on trying to make my life hell.

The dude wants so bad to be like me, he comes after anything and everything that's mine, including my team.

"Hell has a better chance of freezing over before I'll get along with Crew Savage."

Rush sighs and nods. It may not be the answer they wanted to hear, but I knew they understood the history between us. It's too much to be able to easily bury the hatchet.

"You wanna know what I think?" Miles asks.

"No, but something tells me you're gonna tell me anyway," I joke, and the rest of the guys join in laughing.

"I think the two of you are more alike than you are different, and that's what pisses you both off. He rubs you wrong because you see a lot of yourself in him. You're both talented, you both have a temper, and you both want to get your way no matter what the costs."

I guess he is right about that, even if I hate the thought of being anything like that fuckin' prick.

"What about you?" I change the subject to Rush. "They say this could be the time you hang up your jersey. You think you still have one or two more seasons left in ya?"

Colson glances over at Sydney, who's helping Emmy set up the food on the table near the pool. There's food, drinks, and treats galore with blue and pink balloons shaped like little basketballs.

"I'm not going anywhere," Colson says. "I'll be out there playing until my knees give out."

I smack him on the chest, and he reaches his hand out to shake mine.

A whistle blows, and we all turn toward where the sound comes from to find Cody bouncing in, with a bouquet of balloons trailing behind him.

"Daddy Wild? Oh Daddy Wiiiiild, where are you?" he sings.

The guys start laughing. It takes me a minute to realize what I'm seeing when the balloons stop moving long enough. There's an eggplant intermixed with a large "Congratulations" balloon, with a few pink and blue ones to even it out.

I roll my eyes and shake my head when he spots me, bounding over to deliver my surprise in person.

"What the hell is this?" I quip.

"Congratulations on dickin' her down."

My eyes nearly bulge out of their sockets, recalling the first time I saw him and Emmy outside of the airport, talking about the surprise they delivered to her ex.

Sad dick balloons.

Cody hands the bouquet over to me, popping his hip out and flashing me a wink.

"That's exactly the reaction I was hoping for too." He grins. "I knew from the moment I met you, you knew what to do with that thing. Good job, Daddy, for layin' it down."

"Will you quit it?" Emmy chastises him, grabbing Cody by the arm and dragging him over to meet Sydney. Kaylee walks in and waves at everyone before joining them.

"What the hell was that?" Darius asks, coming up behind me, slapping me on the back. The guys all chuckle under their breath, confused and baffled by what they just witnessed.

"Don't ask, please. Don't even ask."

Emmy waves me over, holding up the makeshift basketball bomb signaling its time.

When she told me about her plan to have this gender reveal party, she shared her idea of having me dunk this basketball and apparently when it breaks, it's going to release powder in pink or blue, telling us whether it's a boy or a girl.

"You ready?" I ask Emmy as everyone gathers around us on the basketball court. She's standing in front of me.

I hold the ball under my arm, pressing my other hand to her stomach, leaning in to kiss her.

"I don't care if it's a boy or a girl," I whisper. "They're already giving me more than I ever thought possible. All I want is for them to be happy and healthy."

Emmy pulls back and grins. "If it's a boy, I hope he grows up to be as protective and determined as you."

"If it's a girl, I hope she has your smile and your big heart."

Tears prick her eyes. I've been doing this to her far too often since she got pregnant, I'm beginning to feel bad. I reach up and brush the tear from her eye, kissing her again before I back up.

The guys start cheering me on before everyone joins in to chant, "Wi-ld! Wi-ld!"

When I go up for the shot, slamming the ball against the rim, I'm met with a cloud of smoke.

Blue smoke.

"It's a boy!" They cheer.

Emmy's hand folds over her face, and she squeezes her eyes shut. Kaylee, Sydney, and Cody rush over to her, wrapping her in a group hug.

When she turns back around toward me, her eyes widen in shock when she finds me down on one knee in front of her, holding out the ring I've had since the day after we moved into our house.

If I'm being honest, I knew long before that night or even before I found out she was pregnant that I wanted to marry her, but it was as if all the stars were aligning and unfolding in the most perfect way.

Emmy is all I've ever wanted in a woman; all I've ever needed in a partner.

She's the gentle to my reckless.

The calm to my wild.

"Marry me."

The tears flow freely down her face, only this time she doesn't even bother to wipe them away. She stares down at me before wrapping her arms around my neck, crashing her lips against mine.

My hands hold her stomach, attempting to grip the ring box while silently wishing I could carry her inside the house and have her alone.

She pulls back and presses her forehead against mine.

"You didn't answer me, baby."

"You should already know the answer, Jaxsen. Yes! Of course, it's yes. Always, yes."

She holds my cheeks in her hands and kisses me again before stepping back to stare down at the ring. Her eyes widen when she sees it, looking back up at me and to the ring again.

"I'm going to marry you so hard," she laughs, as I slip the ring on her finger.

"You better." I grin. "Marry me and give me lots of babies."

"We can kick all these people out of here right now and start practicing."

I throw my head back and laugh.

"I heard that," Cody snickers.

This woman will forever keep me wild.

Want to keep up with all of the new releases in Vi Keeland and Penelope Ward's Cocky Hero Club world? Make sure you sign up for the official Cocky Hero Club newsletter for all the latest on our upcoming books: www.subscribepage.com/CockyHeroClub

Check out other books in the Cocky Hero Club series: www.cockyheroclub.com

BONUS SCENE

Dear Reader,

I hope you enjoyed Jaxson and Emmy's story as much as I loved writing it.

I couldn't get enough of their love and wanted to give you a glimpse into their lives, so I wrote you a sexy and heartfelt bonus epilogue exclusively for you. All you have to do is visit the link below or scan the QR code with your phone, sign up for my newsletter, and you'll get access.

www.authorbrookeobrien.com/bonus

If you want to stay up to date with my sales and new releases, you can follow me on Bookbub at: www.bookbub.com/profile/brooke-o-brien

Brooke

PERSONAL FOUL

BOOK ONE

USA TODAY BESTSELLING AUTHOR

BROOKE O'BRIEN

CHAPTER ONE

RUSH

"Get out of my lane, motherfucker!"

Those words, combined with the sound of screeching tires, force my eyes wide open, sending my heartrate from zero to sixty in two seconds flat.

A car swerves in front of us before veering off into another lane as my driver, Jairo, starts shouting expletives in Spanish.

"Sorry 'bout that, boss," he says before continuing to curse under his breath. The tone of his voice mixed with the slight curl in his lip would send chills down anyone's spine. "These drivers are out to test my patience today."

"S'all good," I grunt.

Up until a few months ago, I had spent my entire career playing for Chicago. We had built a team we thought would take us all the way to the championship. Things changed after we were eliminated in the second round of the playoffs.

I was disappointed when I learned one of those changes was trading me to Miami to play for the Blaze. I had begun to put down roots and had high hopes of spending the rest of my career playing for Chicago, eventually planning on raising a family there, too.

Miami is now my home, though. If there was any team I'd want to be traded to, it would be the Miami Blaze.

The Blaze organization set me up with a company to help oversee my move, which took a tremendous weight off my back while I spent time with my family in Denver. Although, here I am, arriving in town with no idea what I could be walking into. My only reassurance came from my new assistant's text letting me know the move went smoothly and according to plan.

"We should be there in about fifteen minutes," Jairo says through the cloud of exhaustion settling over me.

I gaze out at the blue skies mixed with the skyscrapers with the clear water in the distance as a backdrop. The Florida sun blows a warm breeze through the window. The temperature is high, reminding me of the stifling humidity back in Chicago.

I sigh, tilting my head back against the headrest, shutting my eyes, taking a moment to unwind as the city streets pass us by.

A few minutes later, the GPS signals our destination is on the right. When I finally break my eyes open, I'm met with the city streets of downtown Miami. Palm trees line the sidewalks surrounding the building which boasts impressive floor-to-ceiling windows. It's what drew me to the apartment in the first place, and the stunning view overlooking the ocean. A few people walk along the sidewalk, bags in their hands from the shops lining the strip.

Hitting the unlock button, I slip out and round the back of the SUV to collect my luggage when a shriek pierces my ears.

"Get off me," a woman grunts. "Help me! Please, help! He's trying to steal my purse."

Commotion breaks out; women around her start to scream as a man yells at her to let go of her bag and he won't hurt her, but she refuses to give in. Every time he pulls on the handle, she tugs back even harder.

He may have her on a size aspect in height, but she's feisty, holding her own. The fire inside her matches her red hair, and she refuses to give in.

My heart beats wildly in my chest, sending my adrenaline pumping. Where I come from, you don't put your hands on a woman. I imagine her as my mom growing up, struggling to provide for us, and someone trying to steal from her.

All I can see is red.

"Get the fuck off her, man!" I roar, rushing toward him, pushing him back. "What the fuck you thinkin' putting your hands on a woman?"

He raises his fist at me, still not letting go of the bag. I move my arm, attempting to shield my face when he clocks me in the jaw.

"Motherfucker," I grunt, spitting out blood on the ground. "You wanna come at me?"

I charge toward him, pressing his back against the brick wall, pulling her along with us. Shoving my forearm under his chin, I hook a right fist landing a direct hit to his eye. Blood gushes from his brow, dripping down his face.

I don't slow down and my fist scores a hit to his gut. I shove my forearm against his chest and warn him to drop the purse. His hold loosens, sending the woman falling to the ground, tripping over her heels.

Her shrill, pain-stricken cry rings from behind me, but I don't take my eyes off him. There's no telling what he'll do now. Pain thrums through my hand, and a small voice pushes through my mind, realizing how bad it could be if I managed to injure my hand. I don't allow myself a chance to think about it, not right now.

"All right," he sighs, holding his hands up in surrender. "All right, man."

My defenses are still up, waiting for the second he tries to make a move. He takes a step to the side, adding distance between the woman and me. A quick glance out of the corner of my eye shows she's seated on the ground, blood dripping from her knee and down her shin, tears streaming down her face.

"Are you okay?"

"Yeah." She nods. Her chest trembles with the force of her cries, trying to catch her breath.

"Fuck this!" the would-be thief shouts, taking off running down the street, weaving in and out of people. He crashes into one man, nearly forcing him to knock over an older woman passing by him.

"Goddammit," I say through gritted teeth.

"It's okay," a bystander says, holding up her phone. "I called the police and gave them his description."

"Ms. C, are you okay? I saw what happened and called 9-1-1. Police and an ambulance are on their way."

A middle-aged man stands over her, clutching a phone in his hand. His eyes are wide, worried. He's dressed in a button-down shirt, black slacks, and a tie. Judging by his attire and nametag reading "Antonio," I assume he must work in my new apartment building.

"Thank you, Antonio," she exhales heavily. "Would you mind?"

Her green eyes stare up at me as she holds out her hand in a non-verbal request to help her stand. My heart stutters while I struggle to catch a breath when I get the chance to look at her.

Her soft, red hair matches the light dusting of freckles that cross over her nose and cover the apples of her cheeks. Her eyes are green, so vibrant they almost would look blue if it wasn't for the sunlight overhead. I slip her hand in mine, helping her to stand. Pain radiates through my knuckle and up my forearm when I pull her to stand, causing me to wince.

"Oh, God, your hand. It's all bloody."

She grimaces, reaching for my hand. The worry cloaking her big doe eyes wraps around my heart, gripping tightly.

How is it her stare alone has me feeling more off-kilter than the altercation a moment ago?

Sirens blaring in the background grow louder as the cops pull up along with an ambulance right behind them.

I then realize we have a crowd forming around us. Bystanders with cell phones aimed at us mumble to themselves as they point at me in recognition.

It all happened so quickly. I spot Jairo doing his best to keep the crowd of people back, not letting them get too close. He glances over his shoulder, his eyes penetrating me as if saying, "What the hell, man?"

The sunglasses I had been wearing earlier were knocked off my face when everything went down, leaving me feeling more exposed.

"Is everything okay here?" the cop asks, approaching us, looking from me to the red-headed beauty now leaning against the side of the building. "We got a call about an assault."

The redhaired beauty briefly runs down what happened while I clench my hand into a fist, checking out my injury. My head is going to be sore from the jab he got in toward the end, but otherwise, I'll be fine.

"I'm okay," she murmurs, adjusting her position to stand. "A few bumps and bruises, but it's nothing a few bandages won't fix."

The cop looks from her, back to my tattered knuckle. "You okay?"

I nod.

"All right, we'll have the paramedics check you out, and we'll need to get your statements."

He glances from her, over to me, then to the crowd of people forming a few feet away, before asking, "We can do this somewhere more private if you prefer?"

"Please," I sigh, ducking my head back down.

"You got it."

He turns away from us to the other officers, asking the people to step back and give us some privacy. Antonio offers the woman a wheelchair to sit in while the paramedics check her over and the police take her statement.

She shakes her head, assuring him she's okay before she peeks over at me. She puts on a brave smile as I offer her my arm, helping her into the building. We separate while I take a minute to talk with the cops, giving the EMTs time to check her over.

"Do you happen to know the man who did this?" the officer asks.

"No, I don't know anyone here, honestly."

"You just getting into town?"

"Yeah." I nod.

"I figured," he says, jotting notes on a pad of paper.

We run through all his questions, everything from a description of the man to my recollection of what happened. It all went down so quickly, piecing it together again takes me a few minutes.

After we wrap up, the officer shakes my hand and says, "Thank you for stepping in to help her. It could've gone much worse if you hadn't. I'm glad you're here in Miami, and I'm looking forward to watching you play this season."

I thank him for his service before he slips in that he's a season ticket holder and how he's hoping we'll make it to the finals this year.

The paramedics do a quick assessment of my head to check for a concussion. In the end, they confirm everything is fine, and I will need to take it easy over the next couple of days.

"How are you feeling?" I ask, seeing her now-bandaged knee.

"I'm okay." She smiles. "Thank you so much for your help. I can't imagine what would've happened had you not been there."

"It's no problem," I assure her.

She peers up at me over her long eyelashes and winces. If I had to guess, it's from the nice shiner I was told I'd be sporting for a few days, but I'm confident it looks far worse than it truly is.

"No problem? You happen to look in the mirror yet, though?"

"Nah, but I feel fine, and they told me all is well. I'm not too worried about it."

Her eyes travel over my face, down to where my hand is curled in a fist in front of my chest, zeroing in on my cut-up knuckles. I attempt to turn them away from her, not wanting her to worry about me but rather focus on herself.

"How's your knee doing? Need any help, you know, getting to wherever you were going?"

She bites down on the corner of her lip, weighing her options with considerate thought, before responding with, "I think I can get around okay, although, I wouldn't mind you walking with me. You know, for moral support."

She fights back a smile as the paramedic tosses the remaining supplies into his bag.

He coughs slightly, muttering, "Do it."

I glance over at him before looking back at her. A knowing smirk lines her eyes as she shrugs as if saying, "Well, are you going to listen to him?"

"You didn't have to ask."

The medic chuckles, lifting his bag off the ground and says, "Good, because if you weren't going to take her up on it, I sure as hell was."

He turns his attention back to her to give some instructions. "Now, just take it easy. If you experience any swelling, elevate it with some ice. It'll be tender for a few days, but you'll be back to normal in no time at all, I'm sure."

She smiles, her eyes flashing to me, before thanking him. They clear out the lobby area, leaving us alone for the first time since we met.

Refocusing my attention to her, I hold my hand out to help her stand again.

"You know, we didn't even get to introduce ourselves properly. I'm Colson."

"Nice to meet you. I'm Sydney." She gives me an impish grin.

"Sydney," I repeat, letting her name roll off my tongue. "Nice to meet you, Sydney."

"Would you mind walking me up to my place?" she asks, motioning to the elevator. She purses her lips together, fighting off a smile.

"You know, it's not safe to offer a stranger the opportunity to walk you to your door."

"Well, I wouldn't call you a stranger. You did just practically save my life."

She smiles at me as I hold my arm out to her. Without hesitation, she loops her arm through mine, using me as a crutch to help her. Her other hand grips the strap of her purse, where the other end dangles from the side, the leather end frayed from where it was ripped.

It takes a little time, but we make it to the elevator.

"What floor are you on?"

"Fourteen."

"Same here." I grin as she leans against the railing opposite me as I push the button for the fourteenth floor and wait as the doors close behind us. Once they shut, it's as if all the oxygen is sucked from the small space, and I'm left with nowhere to go, nowhere to turn. The slight smirk lining her lips has me rooted in place.

I'm not sure what type of woman I expected Sydney to be, I guess I'd need more time with her to truly be the judge of it, but I half expected her to avoid my gaze the entire ride up to our floor.

That's not what I got though. She used every second of time that ticked by to let her eyes drink me in, and I loved watching her get her fill.

Her beauty, her confidence, even with her broken purse sitting at her feet, her mascara smeared from her tears, her hair a little disheveled, she doesn't hold back.

She doesn't even try to disguise her thoughts or feelings, and there's something incredibly sexy about a woman this confident and sure of herself.

When we reach our floor, the elevator dings, and we step out into the small lobby area. I hold the door open for her as she collects her purse and limps out.

"Which apartment is yours?" I ask.

"1B."

"You're not too far from me." She smiles sheepishly. "I'm new to the building, well, Miami, too. I'm in 4B, at the end of the hall."

All the apartments ending in B are down our hallway, which means she's only a few doors down from where I am. By the looks of it, I'll be making many trips past her place, seeing as I'll have to pass by her apartment to get to mine.

She slips the key into her lock and pushes the door open, taking her heels from me, dropping them inside her doorway.

Standing in the hall, she peers up at me, and a weird feeling comes over me. If I didn't know better, I'd say this feels like the end of a date, only we hardly got any time together, and I still don't want it to end.

"If you need anything, well, you know where to find me now. If you have a cat that needs saving, any fires put out," I mutter, clearing my throat when I realize how that sounds coming out of my mouth.

Why don't you come right out and say, *I'll come rescue your pussy cat and put out the fire for you*, I think to myself.

Insert foot into mouth.

She clearly picks up on where my mind went, chuckling lightly and shaking her head.

"You're a real superhero. You know that?"

"I guess I am." I laugh. When I throw in the wink at the end, she covers her mouth to hide her smile, threatening to split her face in two.

"I owe you one. Once I'm all healed, and we're both feeling better, how about we do dinner or drinks?"

"Deal."

"Great. Have a good night, Batman!"

She takes the last step into her apartment before flashing me a small wave.

"To the Batmobile!" I shout playfully.

I can hear her laughing as the door springs shut behind her.

CHAPTER TWO

SYDNEY

Gripping the bottle of wine and the bag of takeout in my hand, I let out a deep breath when reaching my fist out to knock on the door.

Am I really making the first move right now?

I am. What the hell is wrong with me?

Before I have a chance to flee down the hall, the lock on the door clicks, and the door swings open. I'm face-to-face with those dimples and his cheeky smirk, and I'm left wondering why I was questioning this decision to begin with.

"Sydney." He grins.

"Colson." I bite down on my lower lip to prevent my smile from splitting my face in half. What is it about him that sends my mind and my nerves into a frenzy?

Holding up the bottle of wine, I manage to regain some sense of composure and spit out the words I was meaning to say that brought me to his door.

"I know you just flew in, and it's been a crazy day, but I was hoping I could thank you with dinner. Chinese. Wine. You in?"

"Did you say Chinese?" His mouth falls open. For a second, I worry he might have a history with Chinese food, swearing off it for the rest of his life, concern etched on my face watching him press his hand against his stomach.

"Yeah, sesame chicken and egg rolls. China House is one of the best restaurants in Miami. You said you were new to the area. You have to try it."

"Well, I'm not about to say no to a beautiful woman feeding me the best Chinese in Miami."

He takes a step back, holding the door open for me to pass through. He wasn't lying when he said he just moved here.

"You'll have to forgive me for how my place looks right now. It's a little messy."

He gives a self-deprecating laugh, reaching his hand up and motioning to the boxes stacked against the wall of the living room. He runs his hand over the back of his neck, causing the muscles in his arm to flex.

"You're good. I moved in last week, finally got all my stuff unpacked over the weekend. I'm starting a new job on Monday, so I knew I wouldn't have the time. Not to mention, I didn't want to be left without anything to wear."

Colson's eyes flash to me, down to my denim shorts and white, cotton T-shirt tied at my waist. Something tells me he was picturing what I might look like when I show up to work, or with nothing on at all. His eyes connect with mine, desire flashing over his face. We can both feel the heat simmering under the surface.

He clears his throat, changing the subject. "Well, let's see what we can find to dish up our food."

It seems the realization hits both of us as he chuckles, turning his head toward the kitchen.

"Yeah...let's."

My feet pad across the hardwood floors, through the entryway to the bar lining the kitchen.

He comes around the bar, standing next to me with two plates, silverware, and two wine glasses. Immediately, I reach for my wine glass and waste no time to pop the cork, pouring a heavy glass.

"Sorry, I still feel like my nerves are fried from earlier."

Never mind the fact being around him erupts butterflies in my stomach and the warm zap through my body when his arm brushes mine is unlike anything I've felt in a long time.

For the last four years, I've been laser-focused on my schooling. Growing up, I had a hard childhood. After I was adopted, I spent most of my teenage years living in a sports family. Basketball had become one of my passions the first time my dad brought me with him to practice.

I've kept most of my relationships strictly in the friend zone, not wanting to lose focus on the end goal. I guess I've chosen to keep things surface level, not willing to open up at the risk of getting hurt as I have in the past.

We both take a seat at the bar, dishing out our plates of food. The conversation flows easily. I take in the relaxed smile on Colson's face while his dark eyelashes and warm caramel eyes flash over at me. At the same time, he talks about his recent trip back to Colorado to see his family, and we bond over our decision to move to Miami for our careers.

He makes a comment about how it's been a while since he's seen the ocean, and I make a mental note to drag him with me down to the beach when things settle down over the next couple weeks.

Colson pours himself a glass of wine, but it isn't until I reach for the bottle to pour myself a second glass, I notice he still hasn't touched his. Swirling the wine in my glass, I take a drink, feeling the effects hit me.

"I want to say thank you again for today." I pause, reaching my hand out to grab onto his forearm. He turns slightly in his seat, enough to face me. "The officer called earlier to follow up and let me know they arrested him. I guess they found a gun on him. Just hearing that, I know things could've gone much worse."

"Whoa, hey."

Colson must sense the darkness of my thoughts. He reaches for my hand, tightening around his forearm. He gently slips his hand in mine, stepping down from the barstool, pulling me out of my seat with him. Without hesitation or questioning, he wraps his arm around my shoulder, pulling me into his warm body.

"Don't think like that, okay? You can't let yourself think about the shoulda, coulda, woulda. All right? What matters is you're here and you're okay. We both are."

The warmth of his body mixed with his clean scent washes over me, helping ease the tension eating away at my nerves.

Who is this man? There's something so mysterious about him yet calming at the same time. The way he appeared out of thin air, helping protect me from what happened today. How I feel when I'm near him is both intoxicating yet terrifying at the same time. Now, here I am, in his arms, and there's not a rational thought in my mind that's able to convince me this isn't exactly where I'm supposed to be.

He leans back, gripping my face in both of his hands, turning me toward him.

"I was never going to let anything happen to you."

My eyes meet his, and we stand in place for God only knows how long. I reach my hand up, grabbing onto his wrist, holding on for dear life.

When his eyes flash to where my hand is now covering his, before looking back to me, I wonder for a second if he feels the pull between us, too. My tongue slips out of my mouth, wetting my lips, capturing his attention.

I keep waiting for the moment when he'll put us both out of our misery, but as the seconds tick by and the sound of my beating heart vibrates through my ears, I start to question if it's going to happen at all.

"I have enough wine in me right now, I could make the first move without thinking twice, but this would be the second time tonight I was the one to act first," I breathe harshly. "Are you going to kiss me or what?"

His smirk is back, nearly taking my breath right out of me before his lips crash into mine. I know this is what I want, I thought I was ready, but heaven help me. Nothing could've prepared me for what it's like to be kissed by Colson.

He tangles his fingers in my hair, tilting my head back as his tongue traces the edge of my mouth, seeking entry. This is more than just a kiss. He has consumed me.

When our tongues connected, a heavy moan, which escaped his mouth, spurred me on. Gripping the front of his shirt, I run my palms down his chest, taking in the feel of his washboard abs. As much as I never want to stop kissing him, I know I can't wait for the chance to feel his skin on mine.

Clenching the material in my hands, I pull back, taking in the desire glossing over his eyes. My fingers skate over the hem of his shirt, helping to shed the offensive material covering his body.

His jaw flexes, whipping his shirt over his head, tossing it somewhere near the door.

"Praise Mary, Joseph, and Baby Jesus," I whisper to myself, earning me a chuckle.

"Oh, yeah?"

"Now seemed like a good time to say grace," I clarify, my eyes dropping to his gym shorts and the not-so-subtle bulge forming before looking back up at him.

He smirks, pulling me back in and kissing me. This time he lets his hands rake down the edge of my hips, grabbing the back of my thighs, lifting me to wrap my legs around his waist.

Circling my arms around his neck, he carries me into the living room.

"Is your knee feeling better?"

"I forgot all about it." I smile, holding the side of his face, kissing him as he guides us to his couch.

He holds my foot, careful as he takes a seat with me still in his arms. His attentiveness makes my heart swoon.

While I adjust my position to straddle him, his fingers glide up my thighs, clutching my hips in his hands.

Reaching for his battered hand, my fingers caress his swollen skin before pressing a soft kiss against his injury. He hisses, his face wincing as his hand clenches mine.

"Are you okay?"

He releases his hold before a smile spreads across his face. "I'm fine, I promise."

My eyes narrow, smacking him on the shoulder. "That's not funny."

"I'm sorry." He chuckles. "I swear, I'm fine. I couldn't help myself."

This time when I kiss his hand, he skims his finger along the curve of my lip before grabbing my head, kissing my mouth. His lips trace a path from my mouth to my neck, brushing over my collarbone.

"So soft," he murmurs against me, and for a second, I wonder if he meant to speak those words out loud.

With my body flush against his and my arms wrapped around his neck, he moves me to lie on the couch. He leans over me, resuming the path his lips had made down the front of my chest.

His large hand splays over the front of my chest; his fingers brush over my nipple through my shirt. Even wearing a bra, each flick of his finger causes my nipple to bead through the material.

Tightening my legs around his waist, I grind into him, silently begging for him to quit teasing me. My body starts to quiver when his hands touch my bare skin.

He pulls back, watching my reaction as he reaches his hand out, slipping his fingers underneath my bra to rub over my nipple.

"Oh, God," I moan, lifting my hips toward him. Desire burns low in my belly, aching to be touched where I desperately need him most.

His breath grows heavy, each thrust of my hips rocking perfectly against where his dick strains against the front of his shorts.

He moves his hand down to the waist of my denim shorts, his fingers brushing along my stomach, as he glances up at me. When our eyes meet, I give him a look I hope begs for him to touch me as he says, "I'm going to give you what you want. Don't worry."

Biting his lower lip, he unbuttons my shorts and guides them over my hips, down my legs. I want to ask him about his, but when his fingers are back on me, I'm unable to think straight, squeezing my eyes shut.

"Oh my God, Colson," I exhale harshly.

He pulls my panties to the side, brushing his finger over my swollen bud before using his other finger to enter me. My legs fall open, giving him better access. I reach my hand out toward him, needing to feel him, too. Slipping my hand beneath the waistband of his shorts, he lets out a deep hiss when my fingers brush over the head of his dick before wrapping around him.

He thrusts toward me, rolling his eyes closed as he continues to pump his fingers in and out of me, lightly teasing my clit. Each move causes my chest to heave, every breath struggling in and out of my body.

It dawns on me how easy it is to get lost in him, forgetting how we only met a few hours ago, and now here I am hooking up with him on his couch.

"Hey," he moans, leaning forward to kiss me. "Stay with me."

He must've noticed my mind had drifted away from him. He pulls back long enough to lock eyes with me before kissing me again with more passion and fire than I've ever felt in all my life.

All thoughts and fears are pushed out of my mind because, in that moment, there's nowhere else I'd want to be.

Do you want more Colson and Sydney?

Check out the Personal Foul today at:
www.authorbrookeobrien.com/personalfoul

BOOKS BY BROOKE

A Rebels Havoc Series
Brix
Sins of a Rebel
Tysin
Trey
Madden
Men of Blaze
Personal Foul
Reckless Rebound (Cocky Hero Club)
Tattered Heart Duet
Torn
Tattered
A Heart's Compass Series
Where I Found You
Lost Before You
Until I Found You
Now That I Found You
Where You Belong
Standalones (In order of publication)
Wild Irish

Learn more and purchase your copy at:
www.authorbrookeobrien.com/booksbybrooke

ACKNOWLEDGMENTS

My Boys – I love you more than anything on this earth. Everything I do is for you.

To my AMAZING beta readers – Kristen, Candyce, April, and Ana. Thank you for reading Jaxsen and Emmy's story before anyone else, for your honest feedback, and helping me make their story better. I'm so grateful for you! <3

My Rebels Readers – Thank you for all your reviews, posts on social media, and love throughout this journey. I couldn't keep pushing through if it weren't for you. Thank you for your support!

To the fantastic bloggers and my Rebel Release Team, thank you for being a part of this one. I'm excited to hear what you think of Jaxsen and Emmy. I hope you know how grateful I am for every one of you.

April – Thank you so much for your friendship. We've grown close over the past couple years and I'm so thankful to have you in my life, both as a book friend and a real friend.

Kristen – You keep it real with me, always! It's what I love about you. Thanks for riding my ass when I need it, but also reminding me to be patient with myself too. You're stuck with me forever.

Candyce – You've helped me in so many ways since we've first met. I'm so appreciative of all you do behind the scenes. Thank you for being you!

Amy Briggs and Rox LeBlanc – I've enjoyed working with and learning from you! Thank you for all your hard work on this project and helping me learn along the way.

ABOUT BROOKE

USA Today Bestselling author Brooke O'Brien writes steamy and swoon-worthy new adult romances. She's best known for her sports and rock star romances.

Brooke believes a love worth having is worth fighting for, and she brings this into her stories where her characters risk it all for love.

When she isn't writing or falling in love with a new book boyfriend, you can find her spending time with her family, cheering on her favorite sports teams, listening to ASMR, or binge-watching the latest true crime documentary. She loves rockin' a comfy hoodie with leggings and believes the best days include a good nap.

Brooke loves connecting with readers and hopes you'll join her on her social pages or reader group to stay in touch. To follow Brooke and join her newsletter, visit authorbrookeobrien.com/follow.

BONUS SCENE

Edited by Amy Briggs, Briggs Consulting Inc.
Proofread by Rox LeBlanc with Rox's Reads
Cover Design by Dee Garcia, Black Widow Designs
Version: BMO08042023